JANA

That plague called love.

By Elizabeth Johnson

Dedication

I dedicate this book to God Almighty for the inspiration, love, and the confidence He gave me to pursue my heart's desires. Thank you, my Father, for your unfailing love.

To my family, especially three wonderful boys, Josiah, Jesse, and Jaden who encourage me every day to follow my passion.

And to all those that read my previous books and nudged me forward with their amazing reviews I thank you all for your endless support.

Chapter One

Jana woke from her bed; the brutal ring of the phone had rudely awoken and stolen her from the arms of Tomen. Jana stared at the phone and wondered if she should let it ring, and try to steal some more sleep. However, Jana knew there was no use in sleeping because he was gone again. She felt the tears swell up in her eyes as the phone rang relentlessly. With sleepy eyes, she reached for it and placed the receiver to her ears.

"Hello," she said, as she listened attentively.

"No problem. Tell me where you are, and I will come and get you," Jana said into the receiver.

"Ok, I will be there in forty minutes."

She hung up the phone and slowly dragged herself out of bed.

Looking at the grandfather clock on the wall, she noticed it was a few minutes past four in the morning. Her mind went to her dreams again. If her niece had not called her, she would have still been sleeping and in the safe hands of Tomen, the love of her life.

Jana wondered what could have happened this time because Nina, her niece, always got into fights with her mother. Jana often thought that her sister Binta and her husband were too harsh on their kids. Once she had mentioned her feelings to her sister and quickly regretted ever opening her mouth. Binta had hit her where it hurts.

"What do you know about raising kids," she had said heatedly. "These are my children and I will raise them however I like. If you had stayed faithful in your marriage, perhaps you would have a child of your own too. Stay out of it Jana." Binta's words cut too deep.

First, she had accused her of adultery, which wasn't exactly true but anyone with ears would think she was guilty. Then next, she had rubbed her childlessness in her face, which was a cruel thing to do. Thankfully, there was no one else around to hear her harsh words.

As painful as the words were to hear, Jana knew she couldn't do anything about it. If a friend had spoken to her in such a manner, it would have ceased their friendship but Binta was her only sibling and their parents died one after the other, four years after she was forced to marry Amar. The first to die was their mother Bushra, who fell ill and died shortly afterwards and a year later, their father had died too.

During the funeral, Jana found herself being unable to grieve because she had cried one too many tears and there were no more tears left in her to shed for her parents. She comforted Binta and her kids; everyone stared at her as she took control of the situation because Binta was no use and she was too grief-stricken to help. Jana understood though, because before the death of their mother, Binta had not lost anyone close to her; she had not felt the plague of death until their mother, who was super active, had died from a common cold so to speak.

Being the first child, Jana felt stronger especially since she had been through a lot. Her heart had been broken several times and she had slowly mended it back again, only for it to crumble before her again. Jana sighed after hearing Binta's words; it was all she could do to stop herself from hating her younger sister.

A week later, Binta had called on her with flowers, an apology and a bowl of her special Lasagne.

"It's okay," Jana said.

"No, it's not. I was cruel and you didn't deserve that. I can't excuse my behaviour; I just shouldn't have said such words to you. You, you do everything for me, and all I do is cut you down, especially at times when you needed me most."

"Enough."

"No, it's not enough. I'm a horrible person. You are my sister; my only sibling and I was jealous of you." Binta cut in.

"Really?" Jana laughed thinly. "Of what? You have everything and I have nothing. What could you possibly be jealous of?"

"At first, it was your beauty. When we were young, every boy wanted you but you only wanted Tomen."

"So?" Jana cut in, "You are beautiful too Binta."

"No, you say that." Binta laughed nervously. "I look in the mirror at myself and I am all big and lumpy."

"Stop it. You are being too hard on yourself; you've had four kids and you look good for your age. You are beautiful Binta. You don't need me to tell you that."

"That is always your way; you make me feel beautiful but I know differently. When all the boys gathered at our house, you only had eyes for Tomen and I had eyes for Amar."

"Which Amar, my Amar?" Jana questioned.

Binta nodded, "Yes, your Amar but before he was yours, before you married him, he was mine. In my head and heart at least. He was Tomen's best friend and they came together to see you always. I knew then that he loved you, with the way he watched you when Tomen wasn't around. He wanted you too but you couldn't see. I mean, how could you? You were besotted by Tomen and you didn't notice anyone around you. But I noticed Amar; I saw the way he was around you and I wanted him to look at me like he did you. But I was no one to him, just as he was nothing to you when Tomen was around."

"I didn't know. You should have told me how you felt. I wouldn't have married him."

"Ah, it doesn't matter, he didn't want me. He loved you. I think that was when I started feeling this anger towards you. You had it all, the beauty, the brains, the man of my dreams and now look at you, living like a queen."

"Binta, Mother and Father practically forced me into that marriage. You were there and saw that I wanted Tomen not Amar," Jana defended.

"You could have tried better; Amar was Tomen's best friend. Even I didn't think that you would sink that low," Binta said bitterly.

"But you are married now and your husband is rich. Mum and dad made sure you landed well on your feet. Moreover, the men you talk about are no more. You win. You have four amazing children. I don't have any. You have a husband that worships the ground you walk on. What more do you want? I've lost the only man I ever loved."

"Is that why you were so cold. When mother died you didn't even shed a tear for her, not even for father. How could you be so stone-hearted?"

"I'm all out of tears Binta. If I cry, if I allow myself to break down again, I don't think I will ever mend. Don't you understand. You think I am cold but I'm not. I am just holding it together for you. I want to be here for you. Don't hate me. If I knew how you felt about Amar, I wouldn't have married him."

Binta sighed "I don't hate you Jana." She placed the lasagne on the kitchen island.

"I'm just angry with myself. Maybe I'm the coward and I am taking out my frustrations out on you. I never told Amar how I felt and maybe if I did, he would have looked at me differently. I don't know, I didn't want him to laugh in my face. But imagine if he didn't or if he had thought I was worth loving the way he worshipped you. I mean, things could have been different for the two of us. I mean, who knows?" Binta said.

"Binta, let's leave the past alone. You are my sister; you and your children are the only people who matter in the world to me. All I want is your happiness. If I knew what I know now, I wouldn't have allowed mum and dad to push me into that marriage with Amar. I did put up a fight and you know I did. I didn't want this life that was forced on me but with Tomen gone, my world fell apart and I lost my strength and the will to live. You could have mentioned it to me that you wanted Amar because you would have done me a huge favour."

Binta smiled, "It wouldn't have mattered what I wanted. Amar wanted you not me. Moreover, our parents had other plans for me. They had already made plans with Aalim's family. Our futures were set for us," Binta complained.

"So, you understand that we were both in the same predicament but you are the lucky one: you came to love Aalim. I couldn't bring myself to love Amar and believe me, I tried but he could never fill Tomen's shoes. In a way, I blamed him for wanting to marry me when he knew I loved another. He knew I was broken without Tomen but still he wanted to be married to me - he, his parents and ours wanted that marriage. Tomen was a better man than Amar ever was, but that didn't matter to them."

"But Tomen was the orphan with no money. Amar on the other hand… I mean look at you now. You are living well. Mum and Dad wanted you to be comfortable and not lacking," Binta argued.

"If only you knew the truth. Tomen wasn't poor but even if he was, it wouldn't matter to me. In the beginning, Amar was more a friend but that changed quickly." Jana closed her eyes to force the pain poking through her heart away. Clearing her throat, "Anyway, I don't want to talk about this no more. Enough with the past." Jana felt the sting of tears burn her eyes. She always got emotional when she discussed the unfortunate events of her life. There was no getting away from it but she had come a long way since the day Tomen died. Jana never thought she would live again but here she was, years later, still holding on to life and doing her best to do Tomen proud. She had promised him that she would live for the two of them.

"Oh Jana, I'm just so sorry. I didn't know how unhappy you were and still are." Binta moved closer to her sister and wrapped her hands around her.

"It's okay. It's just the way life is sometimes. I guess that's the deal life gave me but I am thankful for the times I spent with Tomen; I only wish that we had more time together."

"I wish you did too. If I think back on all the hurtful things, I have thought about you, said about you and lies I chose to believe about you, it shames me. I haven't been a good sister to you. I just came to let you know that I am sorry. I shouldn't have said those horrible things to you. My children are yours; you know that Jana. And I didn't mean it when I said you cheated on Amar."

Jana smiled thinly, "It's okay but just so you know, at first I tried to be a good wife but Amar wasn't as perfect as you thought. He did things and said things I couldn't forgive. I had my part to play but he wasn't innocent: he was an evil man. Well, look at me going on when I promised myself not to talk about him again. I hope you understand Binta. It's all too painful to relive.

Thanks for coming all the way here. I appreciate it and I accept your apology."

The sisters hugged and kissed, and then Binta left.

That afternoon was difficult because the discussions had opened wounds that Jana knew she couldn't deal with. Jana wondered why life was so cruel and if her sister was living in a loveless marriage as she had done for six years with Amar. There was nothing to show for it, other than the properties and money she inherited from Tomen's estate.

Forcing the memories of the past to fade away, Jana got in her car and began the drive from her house in Essex towards Victoria station. She wondered what had happened to make Nina leave her parents' house in Manchester. She had often told Nina that if she needed a place to stay, all she had to do was call but she hadn't expected that she would be calling in the middle of the night.

When she reached the station, Jana parked her car in front of it, called Nina's phone from the car and five minutes later, a slim looking averaged height girl in a grey hooded jumper approached the car from the shadows. Jana squinted her eyes to check if it was her niece. The girl took off her hood the closer she got to the car. Looking up she revealed her beautiful hazel eyes and dark hair. Jana smiled to acknowledged her niece, then she noticed that she was closely followed by a tall handsome looking boy. He also had on a hooded top, which he removed on getting to her car. Jana observed his blonde hair and piercing beautiful blue eyes. Her niece signalled to the boy to wait at her side.

Jana looked from the boy to Nina. "What is this?" she asked as she opened the passenger door for her niece. "Who is he? You never mentioned you were with someone," Jana protested. Although she had let them both in, she didn't start the car.

"Aunty, I can explain," Nina said defensively, looking from her boyfriend to her aunt.

"Okay, I'm listening," Jana said, looking at the boy cautiously.

"This is Jon and he is my boyfriend. We've been together for two years. Mum and Dad wants me to stop seeing him but I can't. I tried, he is the only son of his mum, his mum said that my parents are too hard on him and that we should stop seeing each other but we are in love. I can't be without him Aunty. We want to be together, and nobody at home wants to understand that we are people with feelings. So, we decided to run away together. He has no one else to go to and I only have you Aunty. If you turn us away, we would have to live on the street because we are not going back home. Please help us Aunty, please," Nina explained quickly. Jana saw the tears and the love and desperation in both their eyes: it reminded her of herself and Tomen and the pressure her mother had mounted on her to marry someone of her status.

Jana gently placed her hand on Nina's face and wiped her tears and then smiled. She wished she had had somewhere to run to with Tomen. She looked at the boy and smiled.

"It's okay Nina. We will figure it out. First, let me get you both home. We will talk more at length.

Hi Jon," Jana said

Jon nodded and said. "Thank you for coming to get us."

"Don't mention it. Okay, you both need to buckle up. We should be home soon."

Jana drove in silence. She knew what she should do as soon as she got home, but she couldn't bring herself to betray her niece. She also knew that if they truly loved each other, then they both deserved a chance to find out if they have a future together without their family tearing them apart.

The situation was too familiar, and it was bringing back memories Jana wanted forgotten. Binta already knew what this attitude had cost her, and Jana wondered why she would inflict the same pain on her daughter.

When Jana got home, she instructed her housekeeper to prepare separate rooms for Nina and Jon. She was sympathetic to their situation but she wasn't going to place them in the same room.

"Relax. After breakfast, we can then talk," Jana said to the two love birds. "And don't worry, this is your home until we figure this mess out," she said particularly to Jon, so he could feel welcome.

"I'm going to my room. Nina, if you need anything, you know where to find me," Jana said.

Nina ran to her aunty and gave her a hug.

"Thank you Aunty, for understanding."

"Don't thank me yet. I have only offered you a place to stay but we still have to solve the situation and I don't know if I have a say but I will do my best for you."

Nina kept on hugging her. "Okay, let go of me now. Your aunt needs her rest," Jana said, and playfully ruffled Nina's hair as she had done since Nina was a toddler.

Chapter Two

Jana walked into her room, undressed and put on something more comfortable. She knew she should call her sister Binta immediately. However, knowing Binta and how annoyed she would get about her letting Nina's boyfriend stay with her, Jana thought that the phone call could wait until she had rested a little and heard what the kids had to say for themselves first. Although she had suffered something similar at the hands of her parents, Jana didn't want to jump to the conclusion that her story and Nina's were similar. As she shut her eyes and invited sleep, the last thing on her mind was her sister's worried face and she felt guilty for not calling her, but she also knew that it had to wait just for a few more hours.

Forty-five minutes later, Jana fell into a deep sleep and once again, she was visited by her lover Tomen: everything felt real just as it had been when they were together. They laid on the bed together while he caressed the curves of her body with his beautiful manly hands. He didn't say much as nothing needed to be said. Jana could feel his love for her and so could he. He moved in for a kiss and suddenly, Jana felt a tug at her side. She moved her head back to look at who it was and when she opened her eyes, it was her niece.

"What is it?" Jana asked in a whisper, disappointed to have been woken up for the second time today by her niece while she enjoyed a good time in another world. Even though she knew her mind was playing tricks with her by bringing her dreams of her and Tomen, it was better than the reality of her life.

Jana tried to open her eyes wider. "Speak, what is wrong?" Jana pressed tiredly.

"It's mum," Nina voiced in trepidation.

"She has been calling and your housekeeper said mum said she is coming to London."

"When?" Jana asked.

"She will arrive tomorrow. Did you call her and tell her I was staying with you?" Nina accused.

"What! No, I didn't call her and now she is going to have a good reason to pick up a fight with me," Jana said, sitting up and reaching for her robe.

"Well if she's coming, then we can't stay here," Nina announced, heading for the door.

"Wait, Nina, you can't go. First of all, you called me and asked for my help but before I can do that, you need to tell me more about you and erm, what's his name again?"

"Jon."

"Yes, Jon. We need to talk, so I can figure out how best to help."

"There is nothing to talk about Aunty. We love each other, and we want to be together. That's the end of the story. If mum and dad won't leave us alone and if I don't have your support, then we have no choice but to run again," Nina said with tears in her eyes.

"And go where exactly?" Jana said sharply, a little angry with her niece.

"I don't know. Anywhere in the world, where no one dictates who I should or should not fall in love with," Nina said, turning to leave Jana's room.

"Wait! And how do you plan to survive if you both elope? Do you have any money saved? Does he?" Jana asked. She wanted to grab her niece and console her because she understood the harsh realities of being forced to stay away from the person you loved most. But she also didn't want to encourage her niece to be disobedient to her parents when she has not heard what Binta and Nina's father think they will achieve by being this hard on Nina.

"We would manage. I have a few hundred pounds on me and he has a little money too. Altogether between us we have almost five hundred pounds, so we will get a place and then find jobs. I will do anything to be with him but I'm not going back home."

"Okay. I get it that you will do anything to be with him and I understand but I just want you to be safe. Let me talk to your mum tomorrow and maybe I can get her to see sense," Jana persuaded.

"No, I have had this talk with her. She is going to say no because she has other plans for me. I heard her and dad discussing my marriage to our cousin in Pakistan. Dad's brother's son. He is a stranger; I don't even know him. I can't allow them to ruin my life." Nina complained as tears rolled freely down her eyes.

Jana got up from her bed and wrapped her hands round Nina. "There now, don't cry. I know what you're going through," she said and comforted her niece.

"How can you possibly know what it feels like in my heart? It hurts. My heart is in constant pain at the thought of not being with Jon. How can my parents do this to me? Asking us to stop seeing each other is like tearing out my heart. I love him so much; I can't live without him. Please Aunty, I just need them to leave us alone. Help me, help us," Nina pleaded as she sobbed into her aunt's dressing gown.

"It's alright darling and believe it or not, I know very well the feelings you are describing. Love is a plague, sometimes and I wish I never knew what it felt like to fall in love. To feel the pain that comes when those who should protect you tear you away from the one you love. Especially when you come from where we do. The choices are taken out of our hands. I only wish that for your sake you had never fallen in love with Jon this early in life. You shouldn't have to be dealing with this now. Love makes you suffer and I don't want you to suffer like I did. I really don't want to see history repeat itself," Jana said as tears of her own soon filled her eyes.

Nina broke from her aunt's embrace and looked at her aunty. "What are you talking about?" she asked, a little confused.

Jana smiled and wiped her tears. "This is not a story for today, perhaps another day." Jana said.

"No, tell me. Who did you love like I love Jon. I need to know because earlier you said love was a plague. Who plagued your heart Aunty?" Nina asked, sitting on the bed.

Jana smiled sadly as memories of Tomen came rushing in. Jana didn't want the pain. It was enough to go to bed and dream of him but to tell the story was not something she felt up to, because talking about her love would dig up a lot of wounds that were best left alone.

She sighed. "Darling I want to tell you, believe me. But I can't bring myself to relive the past. Please forgive me. And trust me when I say that I really do understand what you and Jon are going through." She wiped the tears on her niece's eyes with her thumb and smiled weakly. "Forget what I said about love being a plague: you deserve to be with who you love honey. I will help you; I'm not promising you the world but I will fight in your corner." Jana smiled and Nina joined her with a weak smile of her own as hope sprang into her eyes.

"Thank you very much Aunty."

"Don't mention it darling. We are all different and we all have different destinies. Yours, I pray, will be definitely different from mine as long as you are sure he is the one." Nina nodded emphatically.

"Okay then. We have a battle on our hands then: one I hope we will win."

Nina smiled and threw her arms around her aunty in appreciation and as Jana pulled Nina to her, she knew then that she will do anything this time around to ensure Nina's life turned out differently. Jana got up and pulled her niece up with her. Placing her hands on her niece's shoulder, she turned her around as they both exited her room.

"Aunty, I hope one day you will tell me your story. And hopefully one day you will be able to smile again. You never smile and whatever happened to you in the past that caused it must have been painful; but, in any case, I want you to be really happy again," Nina said.

"You are too wise beyond your age. Now let's get out of here, I am famished," Jana said.

"Go get your boyfriend. I want the three of us to talk in the kitchen because we need to figure something out. If I know my sister, she will be here first thing in the morning and I need to know exactly whose side I am on when she comes with her boxing gloves," Jana joked.

Nina smiled, "I am dreading it Aunty, my heart is racing with fear. What if she doesn't listen to anything you say?" Nina started to say.

"You worry too much. Go get Jon and let's talk this through first okay and leave your mother to me," Jana assured and watched as Nina sighed deeply before leaving her presence.

Jana knew that she shouldn't fill Nina up with too much confidence. But it was easy to do that because in her heart, she already chose a side in this fight and it was her niece's. Nina is eighteen years old and, in this day and age, one will think Binta would know better.

Jana was sure Binta was trying to do this because of money. The excuse for wanting this for Nina will be wrapped in something moral and religious but at the core of it will be money and status. It didn't hurt to marry rich, especially when you haven't already given your heart to someone else. Jana sighed as she waited patiently for Nina and Jon in the kitchen. There were so many factors to consider in this fight; yes, Nina had expressed that she loves Jon but before she can really fight for them, Jana knew she had to be sure this was a forever kind of love. But how was she going to know that? Or who can tell if any type of love is forever. With her and Tomen, she knew the first time she laid eyes on him that no one else would take his place in her heart. Jana always wanted to be with him, to hear him speak, to hold his hands, to watch him secretly when he smiled or the way his forehead furrowed when he was mad. Everything about Tomen Jana loved and couldn't get enough of and he felt the same about her, if not more. So, if Nina and Jon both have that kind of love for each other, then Jana knew that she would be willing to move the mountains to see them together. If not, then she would have to find a way to talk her niece out of this situation.

Chapter Three

Nina and Jon joined Jana in the kitchen, where she was helping her housekeeper put finishing touches to the dinner.

"You two can help set the table. Nina, you know where the plates are - take Jon with you. We are going to eat then talk later."

"Okay Aunty," Nina said as she set about getting the plates. Jon followed. Jana observed the two as they shadowed each other and smiled. She wondered what the boy's mum must be going through now. Nina had mentioned that he was an only child. Jana felt bad about that and she wondered if she should call someone in Manchester to get word to Jon's mum just to assure her that her son was alright. However, Jana knew doing so would break her trust with her niece, so the least she could do was to listen to what they had to say first and then take it from there.

Jana sat at the head of the table, and the three ate in silence. Jana was not a believer of eating and talking, and often wondered why most family thought dinner time was the time to discuss certain matters and talk about one's day. Don't they know that it is impolite to talk with a full mouth? She just took the time to watch the two lovers closely, and although they hadn't spoken much, she could feel the love between them: the way they gazed at each other and being polite not to touch. But, anyone with eyes could tell that they were both madly in love with each other. Watching them almost brought tears to Jana's eyes, which she cleverly shook away before anyone took any notice.

After dinner, Nina and Jon both insisted on cleaning the dishes. Jana took the time to start a conversation with Jon. She stood by the island in her kitchen

"So Jon, did you at least leave a note for your mother?"

Jon turned, placing the dish he just dried on the worktop

"Yes I did. I didn't write much. I didn't know what to say because…" Jon stopped, swallowing hard because the question had refreshed his worry about running away from home. He knew how much worry he had cost his mother but she had said he was no longer allowed to see Nina and even though he loved his mother, he couldn't be without Nina.

"I just told her I had to go because I couldn't be without Nina," he finally said.

"Hmm, okay. Would you like me to call her and tell her you are with me and that you are safe? If you were mine, I would be worried as I am sure you know your mother must be by now. I won't tell her anything but that. I don't even have to speak to her. You can tell her yourself if you don't want her to know where you are just yet," Jana explained.

"Thank you, I will, um, love to do that myself," Jon said.

"Good, okay should we let you do that first. You can use the phone in the living room and come join us when you are done," Jana encouraged.

Chapter Four

Jon spoke at length with his mum and Nina and Jana could hear the heated argument they were having.

Nina wanted to go to him while he was on the phone but Jana held her back. "Let him handle this on his own. You will comfort him when he is done," Jana said

"But we are in this together," Nina protested

"No, you need to save your own strength for your battle with your mum."

"I know but still…"

"No buts Nina. If you go over there all emotional, you will just add fuel to the fire. He is doing fine. Listen, they aren't arguing anymore." They both listened for a while and things appeared calmer because Jon's voice was more rational.

"Okay, it appears you're right," Nina said, forcing a smile to her face but her eyes were in pain.

"I am right," Jana said. She could see the suffering her niece was going through and she knew the battle had only just begun. If both parents don't agree to let these kids be in each other's life, Jana knew this could break the family apart. And if she was going to be fighting in their corner, then she knew this could destroy her relationship with her sister forever. That, she didn't want but she also could not allow history to repeat itself, not if she could help it. "I know you're hurting but so is your mum and his mum. And I understand how you are feeling but you have to be strong if you want to get through this. You have to stand your ground if this is truly the path you must take to be happy. Remember, you are still young and if your decision breaks up the family, it must be worth it. You can't get bored and decide you don't want to be with Jon in six months."

"I'm sure Aunty. I can't explain it to you but he is the beating of my heart, and I know I am young but we are sure we want to be together. I don't know what I will do in a year but I know how I feel now and what I have felt for him for these years we've been together. He is the one and when you know you know. I know I would rather die than marry that stranger in Pakistan."

"Hush, there will be no dying. I believe you darling."

This was proving to be way too much for Jana. She thought she could keep a lid on her own pain or had had the courage Nina was showing now in the past. Then perhaps she and Tomen would still be together now and she could have saved Amar and herself six years of pain.

"Go to him now," Jana said to Nina, and Nina rushed towards Jon, who had just finished his conversation with his mum.

"She said she will be here tomorrow," Jon said out loud, so Jana could hear him.

"Okay, that means both my sister and your mother will be here tomorrow," Jana commented. The two love birds held each other and looked towards her to save them.

"Okay, while you were on the phone, I spoke to my niece about what you mean to her and believe me when I say she brought tears to my eyes when she described what you mean to her. Now, it's your turn. Tell me why you think Nina is worth leaving your mum?"

"Ah, I can .... I don't know how to express..." Jon began to say.

"Go on, just say exactly how you feel."

Jon was quiet for a moment. He looked from Jana to Nina.

"She's my world. That's how I can put it. She is everything. I am only nineteen and my friends think I am stupid because they are busy moving from girl to girl and having one-night stands but the thought of being with someone else repulses me. I love Nina completely; I know I don't have any money now but I will take care of her. I will find a job. I mean the plan was to finish Uni and we can marry but now that her parents are planning to marry her off to someone else, I think the best thing we can do is to get married quickly and if we are already married, they can't pull us apart, I think. I mean what do you think?" He asked, looking at Jana.

"I think your love for each other is beautiful and it's a shame that both your families are getting in the way. I don't think you should rush into marriage, you at least need a way to support each other but if that's what you need to do to ensure you are together, then I will support you and you can both stay with me until you are able to care for each other's needs."

"Oh, thanks Aunty." Nina left Jon and ran to embrace her aunt.

"You are simply the best."

"Okay wait. My hope is that it doesn't come to that, because doing so will definitely destroy my relationship with your parents and it's the last thing I want but I also want your happiness. So, I will do my best to figure something out that works and of course, we will only resort to this if all else fails."

"I can't thank you enough for having our backs," Jon added.

"Yeah Aunty, thanks a million." Nina added as she re-joined Jon.

"Don't thank me. I will do anything to ensure Nina's happiness and we might be related soon. So, that's what family is for. You two may go and enjoy the rest of the day. Let's leave tomorrow's problem alone for now. I need to sort through some things myself," Jana mentioned as she left the two alone to go to her room.

As Jana laid down to sleep, she soon found herself in the arms of Tomen. Again. This was a regular thing: her way of escaping the pain of his death and their lost love. Tomen stared at her as he laid next to her and their bodies tangled into each other. They said nothing - their love was evident in both their eyes and Jana felt very content. Soon it was morning and the alarm blared into her ears. Jana could see Tomen fading away the louder the alarm became. Reluctantly, she willed herself awake.

She knew what had to be done, but first she had to prepare the kids for what's to come.

Jana had her bath and dressed and waited in the kitchen for Nina and Jon to join her for breakfast as her house staff prepared their meal.

"Something smells delicious!" Nina remarked as she pushed her dark hair away from her face.

"Come sit next to me," Jana said. "Coffee?"

"Yes please Aunty."

As Jana began pouring the coffee, Jon strode in.

"I will have a cup too please, if you don't mind."

"Alright, no problem. Did you both sleep well?" Jana asked.

"I would say yes but you know I can't lie to you Aunty. I'm worried."

"And you Jon? "

Jon shrugged his shoulders as he tried to act like what his mum would do when she arrived didn't bother him as much as it did Nina. But Jana could tell he was only putting up a front.

"Well, until your parents arrive, you just have to do your best to put it out of your minds for now.

Jon took a seat next to Nina as a full English breakfast was placed in front of him by the house staff. His tummy made a loud growling noise to welcome his food. Nina laughed out loud.

"Someone is famished," she joked.

"Eat up, what are you waiting for?" Jana mentioned.

"Erm, shall we say the grace? I mean we do in my home before any meal. I know you are not Christians but do we just eat?" Jon asked.

Jana and Nina quickly exchanged looks.

"Oh sorry, please say the grace. You are my guest."

"Oh, ok thanks. Um, for the food we are about to receive, we are grateful to you God and to Aunty Jana for being gracious to us and welcoming me into her home. Amen."

"Amen," both Nina and Jana chorused.

They all ate in silence.

When their plates were cleared away, Jana cleared her throat to get their attention.

"Okay, in about an hour, both your parents will start arriving and I won't lie to you, they will mention that you are both too young to know any better, not to mention the fact that Nina has already been betrothed to someone else. You have so many things that they will use against you to try to keep you apart but I don't want you to worry. Once they arrive, go to your rooms. I want to talk to them first to see if I can calm them down but, in any case, you are both over sixteen and are officially adults now. So, no one can decide your paths in life for you. Your parents' job now is to only guide you and I will help them see this."

Nina looked more relaxed now. "Thanks for your help Aunty. I can't tell you how relaxed and comforted I now feel."

"There's no need to thank me. We are family and your happiness matters to me." Jana smiled as she got up and made her way to her study.

As Jana sat by her desk, she thought of the many arguments she's had with her sister over the past years, especially when it concerned Binta's children. Most of the time Jana allowed her to win but this was different and Binta should understand very well why she couldn't back down from this particular one. However, Binta is stubborn and sometimes will cut off her own nose to spite her face.

Jana stared into space; she didn't hear the doorbell ring. One of her house staff knocked gently on the door of her study.

"What is it?" Jana called out.

"One of your guests have arrived - a woman called Mrs. Sullivan."

"Sullivan?"

"Yes, she said she is Jon's mum," the staff explained.

"Oh! Where is she?"

"I told her to wait for you in the waiting room."

"Oh Okay. Take her to the sitting room. I will be with her shortly."

"Should I inform Jon that his mum has arrived?"

"No, not yet. I will let him know myself. Keep both him and Nina away for now."

Jana adjusted her dress and took a deep breath. In a way she was happy it was Jon's mum who arrived first, so the battle with Binta could wait until she had talked some sense into Jon's mum first.

Jana walked into the sitting room to greet a worried looking Mrs. Sullivan. Jana could tell from the colour of her eyes and hair that she was Jon's mother. She was beautiful even though she looked like she had the weight of the world on her shoulders.

"Good Morning Mrs. Sullivan. My name is Jana. I am Nina's aunty."

"I know who you are already. Jon already told me. Where is my son?"

"Ah. He is in the house somewhere; I will get him for you as soon as we talk through some things."

"There's nothing to discuss. I want my son and then we will be out of your hair. Sorry he came to you; I hope he hasn't been any bother. Please tell him his mother is here."

"Please Mrs. Sullivan, I think we need to…"

"Call me Laura, please."

"Okay Laura, I know how you feel… sorry, I don't know but I can imagine how you are feeling. These kids came to me for help. I mean, we keep calling them kids but they aren't kids anymore. They want to be together and I believe in their love, so I guess what I'm asking is if we can find a way to support them please."

"Support them? That's all I had ever done until they started threatening my son's life. I only have the one child and I'm not about to lose him. He has to come with me. They can't be together if your sister and her husband do not want Nina with him and I'm not going to allow this to consume and destroy the only family I have."

"We can't pull them apart. Nina means everything to your son. Can we at least sit and talk this through, please Laura? There is a way out of this. They ran because no matter what anyone says, they want to be with each other and forcing them apart can only end in unhappiness," Jana explained

"Forcing them apart will ensure my happiness and in the long run, my son's life. Can you get him for me now, please? This nonsense has to stop."

"Laura, please sit down for a little. Can I get you something to drink? You just travelled all the way from Manchester."

"You can get me my son and I will be on my way, thank you."

"I'm not the enemy here; I'm trying to help. There is no other way to ensure everyone's safety than for us, the adults, to talk this through. Believe me, I know how hard it is to feel like no one understands how you feel. And I understand your fear Laura. Jon is your only child and you are not against Nina but Jon's life has been threatened, so now you are against anything that puts his life in danger."

"Now you see my point," Laura said.

"Perfectly Laura. But the problem is Jon will not live without Nina and Nina is the same. So, no amount of this behaviour from you or my sister is going to stop them from being in each other's life."

Laura sighed, "I'm just tired. I just wish he could forget about her as selfish as that sounds but that's the only way out. Did they tell you that Jon was kidnapped once and beaten to an inch of his life? He was left for dead and I sat at his bedside in the hospital, not knowing if he would live or die. This was after we got a letter warning him to stay away from Nina. I can't lose my son or see him go through another heart-breaking situation like that again. Your sister and her husband are bad news and I don't want my Jon near them. I have nothing against Nina but her parents are both devils. So, now you understand why I don't want your hospitality," Laura explained.

Jana didn't know this; she couldn't believe that Binta could have anything to do with anything that would threaten a person's life. It was her who needed to sit and process what she just heard.

"Oh, now I understand why you are so against this union. But what are we to do? They both love each other and won't live without one another."

"I know but they must if they want to be happy," Laura said.

"You need to help me Laura. I know how this is for you but I have to help. Tearing them away from each other is going to kill them eventually and I'm not talking physically. They will live a lie in their marriages if they get that far. They won't feel fulfilled. I mean, even after all Jon has been through for Nina's sake, he still wants to be with her so much and they ran away together. Let me help. I will speak to my family and if they refuse and the kids still want to be together; we will go to the police and report that they have been threatened. Give me your support, give them your support and they can get through this together." Laura took a seat opposite Jana.

"What you are asking is too much. Jon is my only family. His father abandoned us when he was three months old and never looked back. I myself, I'm an only child and I'm now orphaned. If I lose my son, I lose my world. I will have no one left in this world."

"You won't lose him; I will try my best to see them happy and safe. And I know this is very hard for you but if you join me in this fight then they have one less person to worry about, one less person that is against their love. Please Laura, do this for your son to see him happy. He loves you but he loves Nina too. Don't make him choose. Choose to support him no matter what happens," Jana pleaded.

"This is hard. I promised myself I would do anything to keep him safe and keeping away from Nina will keep him safe," Laura argued.

"That might be true Laura but there are several things that can hurt a person in life. We can't run away from everything that may hurt us, especially if it's an opportunity to be truly happy, even if it's risky. Jon has decided his path and you must now decide yours: to support him or to make his life harder."

Tears clouded Laura eyes.

"You're right. I want his happiness but I am scared that I could be supporting something that ends his life. Then what kind of mother would that make me? A reckless mother. I want to support him and I want his happiness. I have eyes. I can see how happy they are together but this is hard if your sister and her husband are not yielding. In the long run, if they succeed in marrying your niece to who they choose for her, my son will be left broken and I can't allow that."

"So, what if we do something about it now?"

"What do you mean?" Laura asked.

"Well, they are set on being in each other's life and they want to marry. So why don't you give him your blessing to marry Nina? If my sister knows that they are married they can't do anything about it and they will just have to let them be."

"But Jon is only nineteen. I mean, he just had his birthday last week. He is in Uni and he doesn't even have a job. How will he support Nina? And with a wife, his studies will suffer. I mean, he is meant to be in Uni now and look at where we are."

"You've just said it yourself; these kids will do what they want. I will support him; Nina is my niece and like my child. I have enough money to help them both start a new life here or anywhere in the world they both feel safe and you can visit them when you like or even go with them. That's if I can't get my sister and her husband to agree.

"This is a lot to take in and I'm happy that they both have someone like you looking out for them. I guess if you think that they will be safe, then I will support their marriage on the condition that if they marry now, they can't start having children until Jon finishes his university education," Laura said.

"Well I can't promise you anything on that but I would think that if they have not gotten each other pregnant now, they could wait a few more years to start having babies. But really, it's up to them. I just want to help them stay together and not control what they do," Jana responded.

"Children will only get in the way now," Laura argued.

"Or help solidify the union and perhaps soften Nina's parents' hearts. Moreover, you need not complain if they start having children quickly. Don't you want your family to grow?"

"I do but all in good time," Laura persisted.

"Okay, one battle after the other. Let's fight to keep them together first and we will gently guide them through their other decisions later."

"Alright, may I see Jon now?" Laura demanded

"Yes of course, I wasn't keeping him away. I just wanted us to reason together first," Jana defended.

"Yeah, I understand. Thank you for being there for my boy and for making me see sense," Laura said.

Jana smiled contentedly. "You're welcome. I will get them both for you," she said and exited the living room.

Chapter Five

"Oh! You gave me a fright," Jana gasped as she met both Jon and Nina standing by the entrance door to the living room. "I was just on my way to come get you both. By the looks of it, I think you already know what was discussed in there," Jana added, as she raised her brow to question them for eavesdropping.

"Well, not all of it. I'm sorry. I wanted to come in to support you but Nina said I should leave you to it. Thank you," Jon said.

"It's okay. Well, I guess we now have your mum's support," Jana smiled. "I will give you two some time alone with her but I will be in the study if you need me. My sister should be arriving soon," Jana concluded.

It wasn't easy convincing Laura to support the kids, and if she were in her shoes with all that Jon had been through at the hands of her family, she would also be very reluctant to allow this union. However, Jana knew that separating two people madly in love would only bring heartbreak for all involved.

Her phone buzzed as she made her way to her study.

It was Binta. Jana sighed loudly before reading the text.

Binta was not coming alone and this meant she had to fight twice as hard. She was over her head and she knew having Laura, Jon and Nina under the same roof as her sister and her husband was catastrophic.

Jana quickly ran back to the living room to meet a teary-eyed Laura.

"Guys please, I need you all to do me a huge favour."

Laura looked panicked.

"What is it? What is wrong?" she asked.

"Nothing, I just think that when my sister gets here, it will be best if I speak to her alone without any of you around. I want to calm things down and make them see sense and I think you should all go out before they arrive," Jana explained.

"Well I'm not running, if that's what you are suggesting," Laura voiced.

"No, you misunderstand me."

"So, what is it exactly that you've said that I misunderstood," Laura pushed.

"Look Laura, I'm not the enemy. I want what is best for everyone. I think, like I explained earlier, if you are all here when they come, you will push each other's buttons. Nothing will get resolved and these two and everyone will feel the effect of the fall out. Is it really too much to ask that you leave for an hour or so? There's a café not too far from here; you and the kids can hang out over there and when I have resolved things with my sister, I will call you."

Laura shook her head and looked at her son who pleaded with her with his eyes to oblige Jana's request. "Please mum, let's go before they arrive. Every minute we spend arguing is wasted. I don't want anymore fights. I just want to be with Nina, I want peace and Aunty Jana wants to help. Don't complicate things, please," Jon pleaded.

Laura swallowed hard; she didn't want to seem stubborn but she couldn't just run away because Binta was coming around.

"Look, I get what you're saying but… I need to tell those people… um… I need to see them and warn them. They need to know that should anything happen to you, if even one strand of your hair is hurt, I will destroy them all."

"Please Laura, talks like this will not get us anywhere. I thought we were moving forward and supporting these kids."

"Yeah! The operative word is they are just kids and they don't know what they are doing," Laura argued back.

"Can everyone stop calling us kids? We aren't kids anymore. Nina is eighteen and I am nineteen. We know what we are doing and we've known what we wanted for years now. So, mum please, for my sake, for peace sakes, let's go. Let Aunty Jana talk to them. She said she will call us; you can come back and say whatever you need to say to Nina's parents later," Jon added sharply.

"Okay calm down Jon. Let's go but I will be back," Laura said.

"Thank you," Jana mouthed.

Jana watched as they got into Laura's car and drove out her compound. She barely had a minute to compose herself when one of her staff came to tell her that Binta and her husband had arrived. She looked out the window from her study and saw the car pulling into her driveway.

Jana felt a twitch of a headache beginning to develop. Taking a deep breath, she walked to the kitchen to get some pills and water. Downing the pills, she sighed. This was going to be a little more difficult than her talk with Laura.

Binta had a sword for a mouth and sometimes Jana could have sworn that Binta's heart was made of stone, especially when she was angry.

Before Jana could make her way out of the kitchen, she was met by Binta by the entrance.

"So, where is she?" Binta spat out with her face looking like thunder before Jana could speak. The anger on her face had drained away her beauty, Jana thought. She noticed the big bags under her sister's eyes, and her unkept hair. Jana felt for her sister, but she had already taken a side and promised Nina and Jon her support and she was going to stand by her words. Binta's husband, Aalim, appeared behind his wife. Aalim, to Jana's recollection, used to be bigger in size to the image before her now, Jana recalled. He had aged a little more, his hair had more grey than black and had thinned more with a bald patch bang in the middle of his head since the last time she saw him. He didn't look so good and Jana wanted to ask after his health but that could wait until the matter at hand was resolved.

"Please Jana, this is serious. You know our ways and you know everything we do is to ensure the happiness of our children - your children. Nina is as much your daughter as she's ours and I am hoping that you have given her some home truth. She can't behave the way she's carrying on. I hope you told her that yourself," Aalim stated.

Jana looked from both Binta to her husband: this was not going to be easy.

"Well, good afternoon to you both," Jana said.

"Erm before we talk about this, how about I make us all some coffee? I definitely need one at this state."

"No Jana, stop buying time. I know you; I know what you are doing. Where is Nina?" Binta questioned sharply as she started to walk about the house in search of her daughter. "Tell me now where you are hiding that girl," Binta voiced out loudly.

"Stop it Binta, this is no way to handle the situation. Let us sit down and talk things through. Aalim, please speak to your wife. Binta! Binta please come back."

"No Jana, I'm not talking until I see that girl. Nina! Nina! Come out here now!" Binta yelled at the top of her voice.

"Screaming isn't going to help sort anything Binta. Stop being strong-headed and listen to what I have to say," Jana said

"Where is our daughter?" Aalim confronted Jana.

"Oh, you too. You both need to calm down or you can both see yourselves out," Jana said sharply.

"Really Jana? You are going to address my husband in that manner?"

"Yes, sorry Aalim, I mean no disrespect but if I can't get through to you both and you've only just arrived, then you might as well leave now. I am not going to shout. I just want us to talk. I want to hear your concerns and then I will speak for Nina. She came to me for help and I intend to do just that."

"Oh, I see, Aunty Jana to the rescue. Just know, even if we hear you out, you don't decide what is best for our daughter, we do," Binta said

"Really Binta. I thought just moments ago, your husband said Nina was as good as my daughter. Anyway. Let's sit and talk this through and stop this bullish attitude. It's no wonder your daughter ran away from home. You are impossible to talk to."

"Are you really going to lecture me on motherhood? Are you really going to act like you know the pains of being a mother? Do you know what we go through with the never-ending worry night and day? How dare you Jana!"

"How dare me what, Binta? Who are you? What have you done with my sister Aalim; I mean do you two not know that you can't force these things? Let's talk about it. Since I have extended the courtesy of sitting down like adults and you have not honoured me in my own house, then we shall stand around here and discuss Nina's future."

"Nina is my child, not yours Jana. I alone decide her future, do you understand me. I alone," Aalim stated coldly.

"I feel very sad for the two of you. Nina is eighteen years old and she is an adult; yes, a young adult but she can decide her own path in life. Your job is to pray for her and to guide her decisions. You cannot force a marriage she doesn't want on her. You cannot go about threatening other people's lives. Especially that boy."

"What are you talking about?" Binta cuts in.

"I'm talking about Jon. That very nice boy that adores your daughter. You know what you did to him and still after all that evil you rained on that boy, he still wants to be with her and she loves him too. What is wrong with you two? Why are acting like you are not enlightened?"

Aalim laughed sarcastically. "You are joking right; you expect me to give my daughter away to that heathen? Over my dead body Jana."

"At this rate, it will be over your dead body. Look at you, you look ill. Can you not see the state of your husband Binta? You should be calming him down, not hunting down two kids in love. You really need to rein yourselves in."

Aalim shook his head disappointedly. "You are a shameless woman and it's no wonder you weren't blessed with children. Can you hear yourself speak? Amar must be turning in his grave and being thankful he didn't give you a child to raise."

Tears clouded Jana's eyes.

"You evil vile man. Get out of my house this minute," Jana spat out, doing her best to control the sting of tears in her eyes.

"Not without Nina," Binta said sternly.

Aalim paced about like a wounded wild animal, looking around to see if Nina was hiding somewhere. "Feel free to check every corner in my house. Satisfy your curiosity, two of you. Binta, why don't you join your husband in ransacking my home. Go see for yourselves and you will find that they are long gone. I could have told you this at the beginning and helped but I see now you are both beyond help. You deserve each other. I only pity the rest of your kids living with you two vipers. Nina is long gone and thank goodness for that Binta. I may not have children of my own but I will not allow you to treat your kids like your possession. You should know better Binta. You saw what forcing marriages on children did to me. You witnessed first-hand the tragedy that ensued. I can't believe you were going to let history repeat itself," Jana argued.

"Not everyone is as weak as you Jana. If Tomen meant everything to you, why did you marry Amar? Why did you stay when Tomen went missing? The tragedy that was Tomen's death was of your own doing. You came between two friends and didn't have the decency to give Amar a happy life. If anyone is a vile creature, it's you and I won't let you inflict your venom on my daughter. Yes, my daughter. She will do as we say and only what we tell her to do."

"I'm not surprised at anything you say but I will tell the two of you one thing. I may have been weak once but that was then and this time around, I will fight Nina's corner. I will show you my strength by protecting her. She will marry anyone her heart desires. If you do not like it, that's your problem and if you don't stop pressuring and harassing her, I will go with her myself and report the two of you to the police. Nina is an adult and you forget this isn't

Pakistan. This is the United Kingdom. Now get out of my house and I never want to see you two again," Jana ordered.

"Hmm, you will regret this Jana," Binta spat.

"The only thing I regret is being related to you; you are a disgrace. Look how low you have sunk Binta. You are not fit to be called my sister. Now go before I call the police on you."

"Come, let's go Binta and leave this shameless woman to herself." Aalim growled.

"Hmm, I pity the two of you. One more thing. Should any harm befall any of those kids, I will rain such evil upon you two, you will run when you hear my name," Jana warned. "Now get out of my house!"

Chapter Six

Jana had wished it hadn't come to this. She knew there was every probability it would turn nasty but she hadn't expected it to go sour so quickly. This situation was out of hand and there was no point talking to her sister or reaching out in the future. Binta had crossed the line and Jana had exhausted all the excuses she gave in the past for her sister's bitter and cutting words.

Jana fought the tears breaming in her eyes as she stood by the window and watched as Binta and Aalim drove out of her compound.

Waiting over fifteen minutes after their departure, Jana picked up her phone and dialled Nina's number. Placing it on the speaker, she placed her phone on the table in front of her.

"Hello Nina."

"Yes Aunty. What happened?"

"Things didn't go as planned but don't let that worry you. We just need to be two steps ahead of them. Please give the phone to Laura."

"Okay Aunty."

Jana could hear Nina panicking as she handed the phone to Laura.

"Can we come back now. I really need to speak to them," Laura voiced

"I'm sorry, they already left. We have to act quickly; my sister and her husband can't be reasoned with. I don't think Nina and Jon should return here today. Please take them with you to a hotel and I will cover the expenses. I don't trust my sister; she could have a spy watching my house and until I know for sure, I want those two to be safe. Let me know where you end up and I will come see you later," Jana explained and Laura could hear the exhaustion in her voice.

"Okay, thanks for doing this Jana. We will leave now."

"Okay, thank you."

Jana ended the call. Binta and Aalim's hurtful words came to mind and stabbed at her heart and yes, she gave as good as they did but she didn't think that her sister would once again use her childlessness to attack her. Jana finally allowed the tears to flow freely down her cheeks. How vile was her sister to blame Tomen's death on her?

Despite what everyone had initially told her about Tomen's disappearance, Jana believed that he wouldn't have killed himself. They had planned to run away together and the day before they were able to action their plans, Tomen went missing and for six months Jana was told he had died. Broken-hearted and unable to mourn her love, her parents quickly announced her engagement to Amar and they were married three months later.

Jana allowed her mind to slip back to the day she saw the dead rise again. Amar had gone to work early that morning and as usual, had declared his love to her. Jana had smiled in acknowledgment but couldn't bring herself to say it back and Amar had told her several times that he was a patient man and would wait until she was ready to love him in return. But how could she be ready when he had married her in less than a year since they were both informed of Tomen's death. Many nights Jana remembered lying in bed, with Amar kissing her and trying to fulfil his duties as her husband and all she wanted was Tomen's touch. She hated herself and resented Amar even more. He was meant to be Tomen's best friend, so in her mind, her marriage was a nightmare. Jana knew from the day she married Amar that he was no more than a friend to her and yet, she had to pretend that they could be more, that they could eventually build a happy family.

Jana always came up with many excuses why she couldn't let him touch her and as years went by, in some parts of her heart, was the hope that maybe she could forget Tomen but that day never came.

Feeling guilty about not being able to make Amar happy or allow him to touch her to the point where they could conceive a child, Jana made the decision to leave the marriage. On the morning she summoned the courage to tell Amar she wanted out was the day an anonymous letter was posted through her door. When she saw the handwritten note, she almost fainted. Tomen had written to her many years in the past before her marriage to Amar. Tears spilled from her eyes as she recognised all too well whose handwriting she was looking at.

"Tomen, could this really be you?" she heard herself questioning out loud. Confused and unsure, Jana shook where she stood. With all her heart she wanted it to be true: she wanted Tomen to be alive. To know he wasn't dead would comfort her but even more comforting would be if she could ask him to forgive her for marrying his best friend. She didn't think Tomen would take her back.

There was instruction to meet at a hotel where room 229 had been booked. All she had to do was collect the keys at the reception.

Jana grabbed her bag and drove straight to the hotel because she had to see for herself. Her heart raced within her the closer she got and the fear of rejection stabbed at her heart. She knew that she had no more rights to Tomen but it would kill her if the love that usually filled his eyes for her was now replaced with disgust.

Parking her car, she went in to get the keys to the room from the reception.

Unable to breathe with every step she took towards room 229, Jana thought that she would faint as sweat gathered on her forehead. She stopped for a moment to pull herself together, leaning on the wall of the corridor. Jana wiped her now sweaty palms over her dress, closed her eyes and stilled her breathing.

She felt her hands begin to shake; it was fear of the unknown. Then a thought occurred to her that this may all be a set up. What if Amar was behind it all and had forged Tomen's writing? *Nonsense*, she heard herself say. *That can't be*, she thought.

Taking decisive steps, Jana swiped the key into the door with shaky hands until it turned green. Turning the knob, she let herself into the room.

Chapter Seven

There was no one in the room. Jana finally let herself breathe out loud in relief. This was a joke; someone was definitely playing with her mind. She turned around to leave and heard the phone in the room ring. Hesitantly, she moved towards the phone, picking it up just before it went quiet.

"He…hello," she whispered. She didn't understand why her voice was all quiet but she knew one thing - she was a married woman and had no business being here and yet she couldn't make herself leave.

"Hello Jan," Tomen's voice roared into her ears and soul.

Jana dropped the phone like she had heard a ghost. She knew his voice so well and only he called her Jan. Staring at the phone for what seemed like an eternity, Jana summoned the courage to pick it up again.

"Tomen, is that really you?" she questioned in a broken voice.

"Yes," she heard him say.

"Where.... Where are you?" Jana asked.

"I'm in the connecting room, next to yours. Open the door opposite you and come meet me," he instructed.

"Okay."

Everything felt like a dream. Jana couldn't believe she just spoke to Tomen as she dropped the receiver, and more importantly was the fact that he was alive and just in the room next to her.

With tears freely rolling down her eyes, she dug her nails into her palms as she moved towards the door. Her heart raced wildly under her ribs. Was she imagining this? Turning the knob and opening the door, Jana looked up and saw him. There he was tall and beautiful, even more handsome than she remembered. He wore a white shirt. The first two buttons were opened and Jana's eyes fell on his toned muscular chest. Her eyes gradually moved to his face; his dark wavy hair was much longer now. He let it fall freely on his shoulders, his piercing hazel eyes, consumed her where she stood. He was breathtakingly beautiful. Her knees gave way and she found her body almost hitting the ground. Luckily, Tomen got to her before any harm was done.

He wrapped her in his arms and carried her to the safety of the bed in his room.

He didn't say anything, and she was speechless herself. All she wanted to do was bury herself in his embrace and remind herself of his heavenly scent.

"My love," he said as he laid her on the bed. Jana couldn't stop the tears. It was a mixture of happiness and sadness that she knew he now knows that she was married to Amar.

"Don't cry," he said as he wiped at her face. "I'm here now. Don't cry."

"You… you died Tomen. Why?" she heard herself ask.

A sad smile curled around his lips.

"I didn't my love. They lied to you."

"I know that now."

He got in bed with her and they both stared at each other.

"Where have you been? It's been six years," Jana questioned.

"And in all of that six years, I had been fighting my way back to you."

"How do you mean?"

"It's a long story. I will tell you but not now. Now, I just want to hold you if that's alright?"

Jana nodded her approval and he pulled her into his arms.

In Tomen's arms, she felt at home. She could feel his breathing slowing down as well, as they held on to each other.

Jana must have slept off; she had not slept like that in six years. She felt at peace, like she was now where she had always wanted to be. When she opened her eyes, Tomen was staring at her and she smiled.

"Sorry I slept."

"It's okay. You don't know how long I have wished that I could watch you sleep and be here when you wake," Tomen said. He wanted to kiss her so desperately but she was now married and couldn't bring himself to it.

"What's the time?" Jana asked.

"I think it's almost 4."

"Oh! Meaning I slept for 3 hours."

Tomen nodded.

"Oh, I wasted all that time. I have to go; will you be here tomorrow?" Jana asked.

"If you want me to be," Tomen said, getting up to help Jana to her feet.

"I do, very much so," Jana confirmed. "Tomen, if I knew you were alive, I wouldn't have done it. I didn't want to be with him. You must believe me."

"I know. That's why I fought my way back to you."

"Amar, his parents and mine wanted this, I didn't. I still don't. I don't love him. It's always been you Tomen," Jana assured.

"I know my love, I know. Come tomorrow. Use the same key. I will be here waiting and be careful. Don't tell Amar I'm alive. I don't think he can be trusted," Tomen warned.

"Really! Tell me more," Jana pushed.

"Not now, go home and we will talk more tomorrow."

"I was going to leave him; I made the decision this morning before your letter came. I will tell him tonight," Jana said.

"No, wait, not yet. If you do that, he will become suspicious and watch your every move. Come back tomorrow and we will decide together the best move to make," Tomen said.

"Okay."

Jana ran into Tomen's arms again and held him tighter.

"I don't want to go. I want to be with you forever."

She could feel both their hearts beating riotously as the need to kiss each other increased.

Looking at her face, Tomen kissed her gently on the forehead.

"I love you so very much Jan," he said

"I love you too Tomen."

"See you tomorrow," he said and pulled away.

"Yes, see you my love," Jana responded and walked back out through the connecting door and out through room 229.

Chapter Eight.

Jana couldn't believe what had just happened. She had to pinch herself to be sure this wasn't all in her head and touched her forehead where Tomen had gently kissed her.

Reminding herself to act normal, and concealing her excitement, Jana pulled into the compound of the house she shared with Amar. Amar's car was already parked.

Jana wondered why he had come home earlier than usual.

She wanted so much to go and tell him she wanted out but Tomen had told her to err on the side of caution.

Soon as she entered the house, Amar's face came into view. Worry filled his eyes as he walked towards her. Jana noticed that he had decided to stop shaving his facial hair. Not that this was the first time she had seen him looking unkept; it was just the first time she had looked at him properly. He used to be handsome, she thought, not as beautiful as Tomen but he could hold his own but now all Jana could see under his top were flabs of flesh poking out from his sides.

Was she to blame for what he had become? Jana shook the foolish thoughts out of her mind.

"Where have you been?" he questioned.

"I went out."

"Out to where?"

"Why all the questions? I was bored and I wanted to go out. Is that a crime?"

"No, just, I was worried."

"Why?" Jana tried not to show any sign that she met with Tomen and more importantly that she was happy he was alive and not dead. Under normal circumstances, if she weren't married to Amar, he would have been the first person she told the good news to.

"I came home early from work. I saw you didn't look too well before I left this morning and I wanted to come keep you company."

"Oh! Sorry, if I had known, I would have stayed home."

"Well, where did you go?"

"To the mall."

"Where are the things you bought?"

"Do I have to buy anything? I just looked around, bought a few cups of coffee and then left," Jana lied.

"For three hours?" Amar continued to question.

"Yes, for three hours. Is that a crime as well?" Jana fired back.

"No, I just think it's weird. If you are that lonely, I can take some time off work. We have enough money; I don't need to work. We could go on a holiday, spend some quality time together, take the pressure of the city life away and maybe work on really starting our family. What do you think?" Amar asked, watching Jana as she dropped her bag and sat on one of the armchairs in the sitting room.

"Yeah, maybe. I don't know," she said as her mind went to Tomen. She couldn't wait to see him again the next day but that will be difficult with Amar suddenly acting like he can't exist without her. The very thought of Amar touching her made her skin crawl.

"Darling, we've been married six years now. Don't you think it's time you really started to put your heart into us? I want you to be happy and seeing you happy will make me happy too and I think a little boy or girl of our own will help us get there. Don't you think?"

Jana closed her eyes. Amar was being nice, but Tomen had warned her not to trust him and for

Tomen's sake, she knew she had to continue to pretend everything was still normal between her and Amar.

"Yes, I think so too," Jana responded.

Amar smiled happily. He moved closer to Jana and pulled her up to him, then he gently kissed her on the lips. Jana shut her eyes and moved back.

"What is wrong my darling?" he asked.

"I ... I don't, I don't feel so good. I think I have a headache. I don't know. Sorry," she said as she stepped away from him.

Allowing Amar's lips next to hers felt like a betrayal to Tomen and with her back turned to Amar, she gently wiped her lips with the back of her hand.

"I need a lie down," she voiced.

"Okay, you go do that. I think I'm just gonna head back to work." Amar stated, annoyed.

"That sounds like a good idea," Jana responded in a low voice.

Amar let out air in frustration and picked up his car keys on the way out, slamming the door behind him.

Jana stood by the window of their bedroom and watched him drive off.

Relief washed through her as she kicked off her shoes and sank into bed. She let her mind replay the moment she saw Tomen again: his scent still lingered on her clothes and it took a lot for her to remain where she was rather than run back into Tomen's arms.

With her head and heart full of thoughts of Tomen, Jana didn't remember to eat. A deep and peaceful sleep consumed her where she laid. Jana heard a gentle rap on her door.

"Madam," the voice called.

It was one of the staff so Jana forced her eyes to open and sat up.

"Dinner is about to be served. Sir asked me to come get you."

"Oh! Okay. Thank you, I will be there soon," she responded groggily.

"Okay Madam."

Jana didn't feel hungry even though she knew she needed the food. She walked into the ensuite bathroom and splashed water on her face then wiped a clean white towel over her face. She made her way to the dining room where Amar was waiting for her.

"Are you okay?" Amar asked.

"Yes, why do you ask?"

"I was told that you've been asleep since I left." Amar looked from his plate to Jana who sat across him as one of their housekeepers dished his dinner.

"Yes, I told you I wasn't feeling too well."

"Hmm, perhaps. I will stay home with you tomorrow. Keep you company."

"No, I don't need a sitter. I am fine. Moreover, I think I will go out again tomorrow," Jana said in passing.

"Yeah, to the shopping mall again?" Amar remembered where they used to hang out when they were teenagers. He was always with Tomen and Jana would sneak out of the house after school to come be with Tomen.

Now that Tomen was dead, he didn't see the lure for wanting to just hang out at the mall.

"Do you think it's healthy to do that?"

"To do what?" Jana looked up to meet his eyes.

"You know what I mean?"

"No, I don't. You care to explain?"

Silence broke between them for a short while.

"Okay, don't worry about it. Have fun at the mall tomorrow."

"Thank you. I plan to do just that."

Jana ate a little, then she got up.

"I'm full. I will just listen to news and head back to bed."

"But you only just woke up," Amar mentioned.

"Yes, I know but I can't help the fact that I am tired."

Jana wasn't tired but she didn't want to be around Amar while he was constantly questioning her every move. The last thing she wanted was to let the fact that Tomen was alive and that she had met with him today slip from her mouth.

"All the more reason I think you should stay home tomorrow," Amar insisted.

"You need to let it go. Don't you have something important to attend to at work?"

"Yes, but you are my family. You are my wife Jana and I love you. Your wellbeing is more important to me than work. If you need me, not that you will ever admit to it, you know I'm always here for you."

"I know that Amar, you tell me so every morning. You are smothering me. Do you not understand? I already know that you care. I appreciate it but you need not remind me every day," Jana snapped.

"I used to excuse your behaviour. All throughout our marriage you've been cruel and you act like I am not enough. I have given everything to you; I have been patient and yet, six years on, I am still fighting to match up to him in your heart. You have to let him go

Jana. He is dead, he is a ghost and he is haunting you and haunting me. We can't be happy if all you think of is him. You lay next to me and whisper his name; I touch you and all I can see in your eyes is how repulsed you feel. I am here Jana! Open your eyes, I am here alive and I love you."

"I didn't ask for this Amar. You knew what Tomen meant to me and still you forced your way into this marriage."

"I didn't force myself on you; it was an arranged marriage. Both our parents thought we would be good for each other and yes, I must admit, I had always loved you. It's not a crime to admit that. All those times you were with Tomen, I secretly wished it was I you loved. Yes, I tried to hide it and I am ashamed to say that when my friend killed himself, as sad as it was, I thought it was a blessing in disguise. I could finally be with the woman of my dreams."

"He loved you. You were more than a friend to him and you were like brothers. Plus, I don't believe

Tomen killed himself. We were running away, and he never showed and there's only one person in this world that I think he must have divulged that information to. You Amar. He told you, didn't he?" Jana questioned.

Amar's eyes turned red; he was quiet for a moment.

"Yes, he did," he said beneath his breath.

"Sorry, say that again. I didn't hear you the first time around."

"He told me, alright. I was meant to help. He asked me for the car and I got it for him. And truly at first, I wanted to help but if I helped him run away with you, it meant I could never see you again. Tomen was my friend and I loved him like a brother but you, you... there was this crazy thing that I had for you and still do. So, I decided to look out for myself and told my dad the plan. I thought maybe they would tell your parents and they would scare him away. Because already, my parent had earlier informed me of the arrangement for us to be married but Tomen was going to be in the way. I'm ashamed to admit it but I wanted him out the way. I didn't want him dead, just out the way." Amar sniffed in air as tears ran down his eyes. Jana's body shook where she sat. This must be the reason Tomen told her not to trust Amar and here he was, confessing his sins. The sight of him repulsed her even more.

Amar let out a deep breath and continued.

"I feel ashamed that you know this now but I have carried this guilt in me for too long. Tomen died because of me. They said he killed himself but I think our parents might have had a hand in his death and I am to blame because I told them where he was going to be. Believe me Jana, it was the hardest thing I ever did. When I was told he died, I wanted to die too and I have regretted my part in it for so long. That is why I want to take care of you like I know Tomen would want me to. I failed him and by the looks of things, I wasn't much of a husband to you. Now, if you didn't hate me before, I know you do now and I won't blame you. I don't forgive my part in his death but at that point, when I made the decision, it felt like the better outcome for me. The need to have you in my life was greater in comparison. I don't know whether to call it love or a plague but it definitely hasn't brought me any joy. That's for sure."

As Amar made his confessions, Jana's repulsion had softened to pity. He was broken and he deserved all that he suffered but knowing that Tomen was still alive made her feel better in her heart.

"Why tell me all these now? Why today?"

"I don't know. I was tired of the guilt or maybe it's because I have forgotten what it feels like to be happy," Amar continued to lament. "When Tomen was alive, when we all hung around in the mall, those were the days I was truly happy. Now, I just want you to forgive me. I thought marrying you would make up for everything but this marriage is not working. You don't love me and you never will, at least, not like I love you. I look at you now and all I see is pity. You pity me," he laughed hysterically.

"Amar stop, you sound like a mad man," Jana cautioned.

"It's true though, you hate and pity me at the same time but love is out of the equation and I don't blame you. I don't love me too. How could anyone love a person like me."

"You need to stop Amar." Jana could see he was suffering but she didn't know what to do or how to ease his pain. In Amar's heart and mind, he had a hand in Tomen's death but Jana knew that was not true. Even if he had meant Tomen evil, somehow Tomen survived and telling him now that Tomen was alive might make Amar more jealous and put Tomen in more danger. So, Jana chose to keep the secret to herself.

"I will suggest an early night for you and I also think that you should stay in another room please," Jana said,

"I'm not surprised." He said.

"What does that mean?"

"You've been looking for an excuse to leave me and I just handed you a massive one."

Jana was quiet. For a moment before speaking.

"I have to process what you just said, and like you said you and I together does not work and we both know it. What else do you want from me?"

"Just your love Jana, just your love."

Jana shook her head and kissed her teeth softly before walking away from the dinner table and leaving Amar feeling sorry for himself.

Chapter Nine

Jana found it hard to sleep as a storm raged in her heart. On the one hand was her excitement to see Tomen again and on the other was Amar's confessions. She wanted to hate Amar for what he did, she was angry even; however, there was nothing she could do until she spoke to Tomen. Jana wished her life wasn't so complicated. If Amar hadn't disrupted her plans to be with Tomen and caused all these sufferings, things could have been much easier for all concerned. Jana felt like screaming until she felt better but she knew she had to keep a lid on it, otherwise she would crack. Yes, Tomen was alive but for six years she had thought him dead and the only person around to blame was Amar. How could she continue to live under the same roof as such a person who betrayed his own best friend? She knew Amar wouldn't hurt her but then she felt uncomfortable knowing what she now knew. She could tell Amar the truth about Tomen but who would that help. She wasn't looking to help Amar, neither was the secret about Tomen hers to share. That information had to remain a secret until Tomen was ready to come out to the world. Jana wished that the night would go faster, so she could go be with Tomen. She wished she could tell Amar she was leaving for good but Tomen had told her to wait and she would listen. In the past he had always guided her, he always looked to ensure her safety and she knew this time was no different. Who knew what Amar could do if he thought he was losing her for good? Yes, anyone with eyes could see that their marriage was a shamble but she knew Amar would not let go of her easily. For the first time, Jana was glad she had no parents to tell her to continue to work on it and she was now free to leave the nightmare behind and go start her life with Tomen.

Jana turned on her side and looked at the clock on her bedside table. It was three in the morning and still, with all these thoughts running through her head, sleep had evaded her.

Then she heard a rap on the door. She ignored it at first then another set of rapping rippled into her ears.

"Who is it?" Jana sat up straight on her bed.

"It's me. I… I need… to talk to you," Amar slurred.

"Go and sleep Amar, I'm tired," Jana voiced.

"I can't sleep," he laughed out loud. "I can't sleep, I keep seeing his face. He won't let me rest. He… he haunts me. He haunts my dreams," Amar said drunkenly.

Jana could tell he was drunk; in the past she would have helped him. Amar wasn't a drinker but there were times when he had been so off his face that Jana had thought it was because she wasn't reciprocating his love that lead him to such state. But now she knew better: he drank to quieten the thoughts and the guilts that ate at him. She got up from the bed and walked to the door, placing her ears next to the door so she could hear him well.

"Please Jana. Let me come in. I swear I won't make a fuss. I just want to lie next to you. It will help me; it will help these images in my head to stop."

"I'm sorry Amar. I can't do it. I can't help you when you are so drunk. I need time too; you must understand after what you told me."

"Please Jana, I beg of you. I know I did wrong. At least say you forgive me. I was wrong to keep him away from you. I thought I could make you happy but look what I achieved." He swallowed hard.

Continuing his drunken chat, "I succeeded in making us both miserable. That's all I am good for but if you, Jana, my darling, my love, if you forgive me, I can turn it around. I can be a better man, worthy of you. I promise."

"No Amar, I can't talk to you about this now. Especially not in the state that you are now. It's late, I need to rest and I need time to process everything I now know. Go to bed please."

Amar gulped down another swig from the bottle of brandy in his hand.

"If you won't let me in, at least... promise me one thing?" He asked.

Jana was quiet. She wanted him gone - he wasn't going to use her as his healing shoulder.

"Please promise me you won't leave me. Jana, I beg you. As twisted as I am, you... you are everything. Everything I did was for you and I know you must hate me now but it was all for you Jana."

Jana sighed out loudly, shaking her head. She had heard enough. The audacity of him to think because he loved her then it justified his betrayal and on top of that, to ask her to remain in this joke of a marriage was the most ridiculous thing ever.

"Amar, I'm going to sleep now. I suggest you do the same." She climbed in bed and curled up under her silky sheets.

"Jana! Jana?" Amar called.

Jana refused to respond.

After a short while, she heard him drag himself away.

Jana was relieved he left. She couldn't wait until morning to go see Tomen but she knew now that Amar was going to be even more watchful and afraid that she was leaving him at any minute. Bringing thoughts of Tomen to the surface of her mind, Jana finally found peace and before she knew it, she fell asleep.

Chapter Ten

Jana struggled to open her eyes. She hadn't slept very well but knowing that Tomen was waiting for her, she quickly got up from bed to prepare herself for the day.

She knew Amar was going to be home but he was no longer her problem, neither did she feel any guilt for the excitement that danced around in her heart for Tomen.

After a long hot bath, Jana dressed up, brushed her hair, applied light makeup and started to leave. As she opened her door, she was met with a little obstruction, so she pushed harder at the door until it gave way a little. Amar's legs were in the way, and she could hear his loud snore, meaning he came back later and slept at the front of her room. *Creepy*, Jana thought. She forced herself out through the tight space and saw him sprawled on the floor, bottle still in hand. Jana stepped over his body, moving quietly as not to wake him. The last thing she wanted was another conversation over his guilt or another unwanted love declaration.

Getting inside her car undetected, she sighed loudly in relief. As Jana drove to the hotel, she wondered about what Tomen must have gone through and why it took him six years to get back to her.

Walking through the hotel corridor to room 229, Jana's body shook with excitement and trepidation - afraid she made it all up and all that she did and saw yesterday were all a figment of her imagination.

Slowing down the storm that is her heart with a couple of deep breaths, Jana swiped the room key until the green light appeared.

She turned the knob and entered the room. Not wasting time, she opened the door to the connecting room.

Tomen was not in the room; the bed was well made like no one had slept in it. Jana closed her eyes and reopened them. Had he left? Where was he? Where had he gone? "Tomen?" she called out, her voice a whisper at first, and then more panicked now that she wouldn't see him again, "Tomen?" Her pitch was much higher.

"Keep your voice down Jan," she heard his voice as his head appeared from the bathroom.

Jana almost fainted with relief.

"You gave me a scare, I thought... I thought...."

She led herself to the bed and sat on the end of it.

"You thought what?" Tomen smiled.

Watching him smile stilled her heart and Jana allowed herself a moment to enjoy the view that was his face.

"You are so handsome," she said under her breath.

"Sorry, I didn't hear that. Could you repeat yourself?" Tomen pretended, his whole body now in full view. He was already dressed for the day and she took him in, in all of his glory. Tomen was the most handsome man in the world, so it's no wonder she was so besotted by him. Taking her eyes off him for a moment, she kicked off her shoes and slid her bag on the bed.

"I guess you couldn't wait to see me too," Tomen said.

"Well, if you put it like that. I mean, we were meant to meet today right," Jana defended.

"It's just a few minutes past Nine Jan. I wasn't expecting you to come until later in the afternoon," Tomen commented.

"Well, why wait? No one and nothing is more important than you. Moreover, I couldn't sleep knowing you were alive and you were here."

Tomen smiled happily.

"Come here." Jana got up from the bed to meet him half way, he pulled her to him. She curled her arms around him and just then, took in his scent. Tears began to run free from her eyes.

"What's wrong my love?" Tomen asked

"Nothing, I'm just so happy. For a very long time, I never thought I would know what it felt like to be this happy."

"It's okay. I understand. I'm exactly the same. I promise you," he said.

He picked her up and carried her to the bed. Jana giggled happily.

They stared at each other for a moment.

Jana wanted him to kiss her as she was dying for his affection but she knew Tomen wouldn't. Yes, he loved her but perhaps now he saw her as tainted goods.

Jana closed her eyes as she tried to bury the thoughts running through her mind but Tomen could see the change in her immediately.

"What's wrong?" He asked.

"It's nothing," Jana said, lying on her back so that her eyes faced the ceiling. She blocked him out with her hair, afraid if he looked too closely that he would see that she wasn't worth too much to him.

"I missed you terribly Jan. Every day away from you was a struggle. Especially yesterday, knowing you were here but then you had to go. It killed me inside." He placed his hand on her hair and gently moved them away from her face. Jana turned to face him; tears gathered around her eyes again. "I missed looking at your beautiful face Jan," Tomen complimented.

"I missed you too," she said and he smiled with contentment.

"You must know, I didn't marry Amar willingly. My parents forced me," Jana explained again. "Maybe I could have fought harder. I did put up a fight but when I was told you had died; I was broken and I was in so much pain that I wanted to die. Nothing mattered much because without you, I was dead inside. Can you forgive me Tomen?"

"There's nothing to forgive. I know you and, that's why I fought to come back to you. I knew none of this was what you want. I think what hurt me most was that it was Amar. He was my brother; he is the one I can't forgive." Tomen's jaw clenched,

"He confessed to me yesterday," Jana added.

"What! Does he know about me now?" Tomen questioned; Jana shook her head.

"No, I wouldn't do that. He told me you had confided in him about us running away together. He then went and repeated the information to his dad who then told my dad. He gave them your whereabouts. Tell me what happened exactly."

Tomen swallowed hard; he didn't like remembering but he owed Jana an explanation. Sitting upright, Tomen tried to recall in detail what had happened to him.

"I was taken. Amar brought me his car like we had planned but the car was running on empty. So, I went to the petrol station to fill up. That was where I was taken by two men. They pointed a gun at me and shoved me into the back of a dark van. I couldn't see a thing; everything was pitch black. In my mind, all I could think of was you. I held on to your face, even though I knew in my heart that I was going to be killed and dumped somewhere. The thought of never seeing you again was unbearable and I immediately knew that Amar had a hand in it, because he was the only one who knew where I would be. But I was of two minds: he either gave me away willingly or he was forced into it.

"After what seemed like an endless journey, the van stopped. I was disorientated and when they opened the door, all I saw was woods. I closed my eyes as the light hit my eyes and felt a hard punch to the side of my face. I remember falling face first into the dirt on the ground and then they started to beat me: my ribs were broken in six places, my jaw, my nose and I couldn't breathe. I remember choking on my own blood. I was good as dead. So, I pretended to be dead. They then started to drag my body deeper into the woods. I never felt such pain but somehow, I clung to life. I stopped feeling the pain as your face took me over. I guess I tricked my body that this wasn't happening to me.

"The guys began to dig a grave and at that point I had given up all hope. I was going to be buried alive. Then, as though by some miracle, I heard the sound of a car. The guys left me to see who it was.

"I thought about running but my legs couldn't move and I couldn't see out of my swollen bloody eyes. I resigned myself to my fate.

"Then from where I laid, I heard the footsteps of a man moving closer. In my mind, I knew he was coming to finish me off but then I heard the van start up and left. I tried to look up, to open my eyes but I couldn't."

The man bent down next to me, tutting his lips. "Oh! They've done a number on you," he said.

"His face, I knew very well. He used to be the head of security for my dad, when my parents were still alive. And then he started working for Amar's dad a few years after Amar's dad took me in as his ward. He literally picked me up and placed me in the back of his car. I wanted to say thank you but I could not speak. I thought I was dead and here was this man. I didn't know if he was taking me to do more harm or if God had sent me help.

"My head was hurting bad when we eventually arrived at his home. It was like a farmhouse in the country somewhere close to the beach. He looked after me, cleaned my wounds and then took me to a nearby hospital. Before taking me, he asked me to say that I was attacked by a gang and I had to give them a false name. He said that if I didn't, I was putting his life in danger because Amar's dad would know that I was still alive." Tomen stopped for a moment and he looked at Jana, whose face expressed horror at the things he told her.

"Excuse me for a moment." Tomen got up and poured himself a glass of water. Jana couldn't move. She didn't know how anyone could be so evil and why it was that Amar's dad wanted Tomen dead. It couldn't all be because of her.

"I don't get it. Why did they want you dead? He practically raised you after your parents' tragic accident."

"I'm beginning to think my parents' death wasn't an accident."

"How do you mean?"

"The man who saved me told me my dad and Amar's dad were business partners and they had been friends from their youth. But when they argued about some things, they couldn't agree on a way forward together, so my dad decided to split from the partnership. Amar's dad initially agreed but when he saw how lucrative my dad's ideas were and the amount of money my dad made, he wanted back in. My dad refused but since they were friends since childhood and Amar's dad was my godfather, my dad tried to help him set up his own business using his ideas that worked. Somehow, Amar's dad ran his business into the ground and became jealous of my dad's progress. I think he came across my dad's will, which state that in the event of my parents' deaths, I was to inherit everything but if my parents died and I was still under the age of twenty-one, Amar's dad was to look after my estate until I was age appropriate. However, if an unfortunate event such as my death occurred before I turned twenty-one, then all the money goes to his friend and his family. In this case, that friend was Amar's dad. Omar, that's the name of the man that saved me. He said he started working for Amar's dad when he suspected foul play in my parents' deaths but he couldn't prove it, so he wanted to ensure I was okay. When he heard what they were planning to do to me, he pretended to go along with it but he almost arrived too late. I should have known that Amar was obsessed with you. He is like his father, always wanting what was not his. I once saw a book in his room, where he had drawings of your face plastered all over it. When I confronted him, he said you were his friend and there was nothing more to it. I shrugged it off and thought it was just because he liked you. I wouldn't have thought he wanted me out of the way so he could marry you.

"So, now that I am back from the dead, I need to get my money back from his family and if you still want me, I need you back in my life as well."

Chapter Eleven

"Of course, it's always been you Tomen. I will go now and tell Amar I want a divorce. I can't bear to be married to him again, especially after what I know now."

"I got a lawyer; he will serve them this morning. I am taking them to court and getting every penny back. Then you and I can get married like we were meant to have done," Tomen said.

Jana smiled excitedly. "Promise?"

Tomen turned to look at her and she could see what she meant to him in his eyes.

"You still don't know what you mean to me by now. Jan, you are my world. Of course, I want to marry you and no one else," Tomen assured her.

Then suddenly, Jana's excitement turned into worry.

"What if they try to kill you again or what if Amar refuses to divorce me. They can do that you know to try to keep us apart," Jana said, her voice filled with trepidation.

"No, listen to me Jan. I have thought about all of this. I will only show my face in court and you don't need to go back home to Amar if you are fearful for your life. He and his father are going to be arrested for attempted murder. Omar already went with me to the police. They can't get away it - not this time. I'm glad I don't have to convince you of Amar's part in all of this. He told you himself, so you know I'm not lying."

"I believe you and I never thought you were lying."

"I'm just saying, just in case you have any doubt in you."

"Tomen, you never lied to me in the past and I don't think you will start now and yes, I don't want to go back to Amar because he creeps me out. He never wants me out of his sight. I just want this nightmare of a marriage over."

"It is settled then. You don't have to go back; you don't even have to see him again if you don't want to. The easiest way to do this is to have him declare that he divorces you three times. How likely do you think that is possible?"

"I don't know. I can get him to talk if I threaten him with what he told me but I'm not sure - he is obsessed with me Tomen but I don't want to be with him. Last night, even after I told him to sleep in a separate room, he came back and slept in front of my door, he was so drunk. There's no telling what he will do to keep me with him," Jana complained.

"Then you don't have to go back if it's that uncomfortable. I will handle it. You can stay in the connecting room and I will call the lawyer to come help sort out the divorce papers. Don't worry, he will sign it or go to prison for a very long time."

Jana threw her arms around him as she felt liberated.

"You don't know what this means to me - this feels like a dream. You and I will get to be together at last," Jana said happily, pulling Tomen down on his back, so they both laid back down on the bed. They stared at each other and Tomen wiped the tears spilling down Jana's eyes.

"You have to stop crying Jan. The nightmare will be over soon."

Jana smiled.

"But this time, these are tears of joy."

Tomen half smiled.

"I'm glad."

"Kiss me Tomen or don't you want to?"

"I do. I'm just waiting for the moment you are mine."

"I've always been yours," Jana argued.

"I know that too but at this moment, you are tied to Amar. I will cut those ties and then we can do whatever we like but not now."

In a way, Jana was glad for his explanation, even though the need to be kissed by Tomen was so great. She felt better inside now because Tomen wasn't looking at her like damaged goods as she had thought before.

"Have you had breakfast?" Tomen asked.

Jana shook her head.

He looked at his watch. "It's almost noon now. How did that happen? Three hours passed and I never felt it."

Jana chuckled. "It's because we are together."

"I know," Tomen chuckled lightly. "I have missed watching you smile," he added.

"I missed your scent; I missed the crease on your forehead when you worry or you're thinking of a plan. I missed looking at you in a crowd and smiling to myself, thinking what did I do to deserve you. I kept waiting for you to turn around and say we were over but each time you showered me with more love and I felt like I won the jackpot all over again. I never took your love for granted Tomen but most of all, I missed kissing you, touching you and curling my body around yours. You are my safe place Tomen; you are my home."

Tomen pulled her closer and at first, he planted a gentle kiss on her lips with his eyes closed -he felt Jana's lips curl around his. The passion between them grew with great intensity. Throwing all caution away. Tomen moved his lips more passionately around Jana's. He felt Jana's body pressed hard against his, causing the fire of their love to ignite all through his body. Jana moved on top of him and began to peel off her clothes.

"No," Tomen said, his breathing rough.

"No, please Jan," Tomen begged.

"Why? I want you, I need you Tomen."

"I do too but you are still married. Kissing is one thing but if we do this, I'm just not comfortable doing this now. Please say you understand my love," Tomen pleaded.

Jana climbed down from on top of him, sighing loudly. "When you put it like that…"

"I'm sorry Jan," Tomen apologised.

"No need to apologise. I get it." Jana smiled. "Shall I order us some food; we should go out for lunch but I don't want us to risk being spotted together now. We need to maintain the element of surprise for everything I've planned to go smoothly."

"Yes, I understand. So, room service it is," Jana agreed. Tomen smiled and kissed her gently on the forehead before going to order their lunch.

Chapter Twelve

Jana remained with Tomen for two weeks and she watched him go into meetings with his lawyers. Twice, she met with a lawyer to discuss the divorce proceedings like Tomen had promised. Amar signed the divorce petition and applied for a consent order to ensure a complete break from Jana. At first, he had protested, requesting to see Jana before doing anything but he wasn't left with much of a choice. The two men who beat up Tomen at the request of Amar's father were arrested and, in their statements, they implicated Amar and his father.

Jana begged Tomen to make sure Amar and his father were imprisoned according to law but Tomen said that Amar's father begged to settle out of court. Every property that belonged to his father had been transferred back into his name, including the compound Jana shared with Amar.

Things were going smoothly, for them. Almost too smoothly Jana mentioned to Tomen when he returned with the Decree Nisi certificate. A few weeks later, Tomen had casually dropped the paper on her lap while they relaxed after their evening meal.

"The lawyer brought this today. We just have to wait now to apply for the Decree Absolute but we can make plans to be married as soon as the certificate arrives."

"Really?"

"Yes, we start afresh and erase the six years from our memories like a bad dream," Tomen said, kissing her gently on the neck. Jana moaned softly.

"I want to begin preparation for our wedding. I'm so excited."

"Who do you want to invite? Same family members that forced you into that marriage with Amar?" Tomen asked, looking up.

"Yeah, you're right. Let's just go to the registry and get a date."

"Hmm, I like that very much. I can't wait to do very bad things to you," Tomen teased.

Jana laughed out loud.

"You need deliverance Tomen."

"No, it's too late for me. Only you can deliver me now Jan."

"Oh. I can't wait to become your wife. I mean, I never dreamt I will be here lying in your arms. You know that many people dream about becoming doctors, lawyers, astronauts, being famous but you Tomen, you are my one big dream. You are my wealth, my fame and to spend the rest of my life with you is all I want."

Tomen's eyes clouded over with tears because he was moved by Jana's words.

"Never ever have I felt so loved by another and you are my greatest dream Jan. I promise you that as long as I have my life, in this world and the next, and the many more lives we may live, I will love you and I will keep you safe."

Once again, their bodies entwined as they began to kiss passionately, breathing hard in unison as with each touch and with each kiss, their love for each other was translated across to one another. Finally, they pulled away from each other.

Jana laughed softly. "We have to stop doing this to each other. It's too hard."

"I know. I wish this stupid divorce was over already," Tomen chuckled gently.

He turned on his back, resisting the temptation to kiss her more.

No words were said between them for a while, then he turned and looked at her.

"I wrote my will today."

"You what?"

"Yeah! You know, I pray that all goes well but in case something happens to me, I want you to be well looked after. I mean, it's just a precaution you know."

"But Tomen, I understand your thinking but I don't want these negative thoughts."

"I know Jan but like I said, it's just a precaution. Amar didn't go to prison because I had a deal with him for him to release you from your marriage in exchange for his freedom. He and his family are penniless now, since they've been living on my money but still, I have to take precautions to make sure you get everything in case I die. There's no saying what they will do later."

"Please don't talk like that. Don't use the word die. If you die, I will kill myself too."

"No Jan, that's stupid. If something were to happen to me, you have to live for the two of us or they win. They get their way."

"There's no life without you Tomen. I was a living corpse before and your return brought life back to me. I couldn't do it again, please don't make me."

"This is ridiculous Jan, you can't die. I won't permit it," Tomen declared.

"But you will be dead and there's nothing much you can do about it then," Jana argued back.

"Promise me you won't do or say anything as foolish as that again," Tomen pushed.

Jana was quiet but she could tell by Tomen's eyes he was waiting for her reply. "I promise but you have to promise not to die."

"I will do my best," Tomen finally smiled.

"That was why I told you not to settle out of courts. They already tried to kill you once and they are going to try again," Jana argued with concern.

"Jan, Jan, calm down. Listen to me, they can try but this time I have people watching over me. Omar has put together a security detail: the best of the best he says they are. If they try anything again, they will be caught and imprisoned okay my love," Tomen assured, reaching out to pull Jana's hair from her face and tucking it behind her ears.

Jana nodded but worry still creased her forehead.

"You don't believe me?" Tomen added.

"I do, I just worry that as long as they are out there, they won't stop. Amar won't just walk away. He is obsessed with me, so he might try to hurt you and this time, I don't think I would mend if anything at all happened to you. I'm no good without you Tomen. I won't survive it."

Tomen pulled her in for an embrace to comfort her.

"Don't worry, he won't be able to get you or me. He won't dare, I promise you," Tomen said with certainty.

"Okay, if you believe so then I will too," Jan said but, in her heart, she didn't fully believe they were safe.

"For sanity's sake, I will go to sleep in my room now," Tomen said and made to kiss her on her forehead.

"No please stay. I won't do anything. I just want to lie on the same bed," Jana pleaded.

Tomen looked reluctant.

"Please, I will keep my hands to myself," she pressed and he smiled.

"Okay. I will stay."

Jana smiled. Tomen tucked himself into bed with her, keeping a safe distance. He leaned over and kissed her on her forehead.

"Goodnight Tomen."

"Goodnight my love," Tomen responded

He closed his eyes for a moment but he could feel Jana's eyes on him, and when he opened his eyes, she had shut hers. He smiled because his heart was full and so was his world.

Chapter Thirteen

Seven weeks breezed past and they went house hunting and bought a seven-bedroom mansion to start their family in and employed new staff for their new home. The certificate for the Decree Absolute had been issued and Jana was now free to remarry again. Without wasting time, Jana and Tomen remarried at the registry of their council town hall, with Omar and his wife as their only witnesses.

Binta was not invited because she had rained abuse on her sister when Amar had visited her to complain about Jana leaving him.

Now home alone in their new home, with all the well-wishers gone and all the staff sent to their homes for the night, Jana excused herself to prepare for the night. For some reason, she felt nervous and had to calm herself down. After all, she was now married to the man of her dreams.

Dressed in a white silk slip covered in lace, Jana gently brushed her hair. She didn't notice Tomen standing by the entrance door to their room.

"You look stunning my wife," Tomen complimented. Jana's tummy flipped with excitement and nerves. She had waited for this moment all her life. The day she would submit to every desire and craving that comes with loving Tomen.

"What are you doing so far away from me husband?" she asked softly.

Tomen chuckled lightly.

Taking decisive steps towards his wife, "I love it when you call me that."

Jana smiled.

Breathing out loud, the closer he got to his wife, Jana looked away shyly.

Tomen lifted his hands to her face and pulled her face towards his.

"I love you so much," he said and kissed her gently, first on the lips and then on her neck, and gently pushed down the strap of her slip so that nothing was in the way of her skin. Then he picked her up and laid her on the bed with him. He could hear Jana's breathing; it was rough and so was his but he took caution to slow down his racing heart. Tomen wanted the night to be special for the two of them, so he gently began to kiss his wife and she responded with much vigour, wrapping her legs around him.

"Slow down my love, we have all night," he teased.

"Don't blame me, I've waited too long for you," she said.

They both smiled but soon resumed kissing as the warmth of her bare body against his quickly ignited an unstoppable flame within him. Tomen couldn't help himself and it seemed Jana couldn't get enough of him either as they melted into each other repeatedly, coming up for air and going back for more. Their home was filled with echoes of their love and for two good nights, with every passionate and divine lovemaking, Jana was convinced they had made a baby.

"You were worth the wait," Jana finally said after another day of multiple lovemaking sessions.

Tomen laughed.

"I'm exhausted." They both shared a laugh. "But I can't get enough of you."

"Same here."

"I'm famished, when are the staff due back?"

"Tomorrow, I think."

"Ah! Okay, I'm going to have to make us dinner then," Tomen said.

"No, I'll do the cooking," Jana said, getting up.

"Hey! Where are you going," Tomen said, planting another passionate kiss on his wife's lips." She giggled.

"I said I'll cook. I learned a thing or two when I was away you know. I can throw down; you just wait and see," Tomen said, getting up.

"What are you going to make us?"

"Beef curry and cardamom rice."

"Mmm hmm, that sounds yummy. Okay, off you go."

"Yeah! I'm just going to nip down to the local butchers to get a good cut of meat. Won't be long my queen."

"Yeah, I'll be waiting for that and some dessert," Jana said, stripping him down with her eyes.

"I've made a monster out of you Jan," Tomen said, shaking his head happily as he went.

Jana got up from bed, put on her dressing gown and ran to the door to meet Tomen before he left their home.

"Hurry back to me," she said, locking lips with him before he left.

"Sure my love." Tomen smiled, got into his car and Jana watched as he drove off.

She rushed into the bathroom to wash herself, examined her face in the mirror, where she could see her skin and her eyes glowing.

This was the happiest she had ever been, she noted.

Jana ran a hot bath and dipped herself inside.

Thirty minutes later, she heard footsteps or so she thought.

"Tomen, is that you?" she called but didn't hear a response.

Jana got out of the bath and put on her robe.

"Tomen, are you back?"

Still there was no response but she was sure she had heard the creaking of a door and footsteps.

Jana felt the hairs on the back of her neck stand up. There was a scent lingering in the air and it wasn't Tomen's and before she could call out his name, Amar appeared with a bloody knife.

Jana's blood ran cold. She couldn't move.

"What did you do? What have you done? Where is Tomen? Where is Tomen?" she screamed.

Amar wiped the knife on his sleeve.

"Hush, hush now."

Jana felt a hot stream of water run down her legs. She had wet herself out of fear.

"How did you enter?"

"It doesn't take much to be a genius. I took Omar's son and his wife gave me access to your home. It was simple really, your lives for her son's," Amar said, enjoying the horror on Jana's face.

"Did you hurt him? Whose blood is that you evil man."

"You didn't think the two of you could get away with it, did you? Do you know the agony I felt, listening to you mount each other over and over again? I mean, you are like a dog in heat. Tomen more! Tomen please more. You made me feel sick to my stomach." Amar made a gagging noise as covered his ears with his bloody hands. "It was torture hearing you screaming for more. I didn't know you had such passion in you. You definitely didn't honour our marriage; you wouldn't even let me touch you. Cringing each time, I came near you, yet, I was patient. I waited, hoping that one day you would get over your sickness for him. I guess I was the fool. I should have taken you at every turn and made you yell for me to stop. You denied me my right as your husband and I won't be denied any longer."

"I divorced you. You are no longer my husband."

"But I didn't divorce you. In my heart, you are mine," Amar spat out and then laughed out loud.

"This here is your fault." He pointed the bloody knife at her. "I didn't plan any of this. I just wanted to come and see you. I don't know why but I am drawn to you and this need for you is like a disease. It's all your fault, you…" he chuckled bitterly. "You won't leave my head; it's like you are imprinted forever in my head and on my mind. I missed you and I can't move on without you."

"I don't care about you Amar. I never loved you. Why won't you just go away?"

Amar looked down in sadness.

"I can't go away because you are my wife."

"No, I'm not. I'm free of you and your evil family," Jana said with greeted teeth.

"No, I decide that, not you. I say when I'm done with you. I am not free of you and if I'm not, you can't be done."

"You are crazy. Do you hear me, get it into your head Amar I don't love you, I love my husband Tomen. Where is he? Where is Tomen," Jana asked as tears blinded her sight.

Amar moved closer; Jana stepped backwards from him. There was nowhere to run to and he had her in a corner.

"Take me to my husband."

Making a tutting sound, Amar said, "But I'm your husband Jana. That man, whose blood is on this knife, he is the imposter." Taking a quick step, he was at her side. He pinned her to the wall, holding her throat with one hand and ran the knife over her face with the other. Jana shook where she stood. She was afraid but needed him to know she would die before she lets him near her.

"I can end you now, and finally, your death will bring peace to my heart." he stated.

"I'm not afraid of you," she stated.

Amar laughed. "Says the person who just pissed her pants." He leaned into her with his bloody knife tracing her bosom down to her stomach and took a whiff of her scent.

"Yeah, there's that smell that drives me nuts. Let's play a game - why don't you kiss me, slowly and with as much vigour as you did with Tomen and then after that, we make love and you please me, just like you did with him and then I will take you to him. With any luck, he may still be alive. You see, I stabbed him multiple times and he is somewhere in this house but

I made sure he will be no trouble. He can't disturb us, so it's just you and I now Jana."

"I hate you Amar: you are the devil's son and I will die first before I let you anywhere near me."

Amar shut his eyes and shook his head. "I guess I expected you to say that." He lifted the knife up but Jana kicked him between his legs and pushed him out of her way.

Running away, she followed the blood trail she saw on the floor.

"Tomen! Tomen where are you?" she yelled.

"You evil woman, I will kill you!" Amar shouted, chasing after her.

Jana was met with a pool of blood by the entrance of the door and saw bloody drag marks leading into a room. Jana quickly followed the marks and pushed the door open; Tomen was holding the side of his tummy but the blood was pouring out. At first in shock, Jana watched in horror as the man she loved was dying but then Amar's voice sounded very close so she decided to barricade the door quickly. Jana closed the door and pushed a chair against the handle. She ran to Tomen; she could see he had been stabbed in his shoulders and his back as well. If he survived this, it would be a miracle.

She quickly pulled off the sheets from the bed and wrapped it around Tomen's stomach. He coughed out blood. Amar pushed on the door to get in but the barricade held strong.

"Please don't die," Jana whispered. "I will get help." Jana made to go but Tomen held her back.

"No, he will hurt you. I don't… I don't think…" he started to say.

"Don't talk."

"No… My love, let me speak."

Jana couldn't believe this was happening: she was about to lose the man she loved for the second time.

"Please Tomen, don't. I can't lose you again. You can't die. Please, just stay with me."

"Jan, I love you. Promise me you will get out of here. Go out through the window and get away from here."

"No Tomen, I can't. I can't leave you. Please don't make me."

"If you stay… he will, kill you too." Tomen coughed out more blood and he knew he was holding on to life for her sake.

"No, I would rather die. I can't do it again Tomen."

"You… you promised me… remember. You promised me that you would stay alive. Live for the two of us."

"No, I can't. Don't make me do this. I will kill myself if you die. Stay with me."

Tears spilled from Tomen's eyes.

"I want to my love, so much. I will… never leave you. But please save yourself, live for me," Tomen pleaded.

Just then, Amar forced his way inside the room and Jana jumped in front of Tomen to protect him from Amar.

"Please Amar, I beg you to leave us alone. He is already dying. Please. Haven't you done enough harm?"

"No! You two stripped my family of everything we had, he took you my wife away from me and you think this is enough? No. He can get to watch as I take you in front of him," Amar said waving his knife.

"You think I'm afraid of death?" Jana said.

"You may be willing to die; I don't care but you can meet your maker after I am finished with you."

"Get…away from her," Tomen commanded

Amar laughed out loudly.

"You still think you have a say in this."

Tomen pulled himself up. "Get behind me Jan."

"No!"

"Now!" he ordered.

Jana moved behind Tomen and Amar swung his knife to deal Tomen one last blow. However, Tomen held Amar's hand and they wrestled on the ground until the knife was loose from Amar's grip. Amar punched Tomen repeatedly in his injuries; blood spurted out of Tomen's mouth and his eyes rolled to the back of his head. Jana picked up the chair and shattered it on Amar's head, who then fell to the ground unconscious. It gave Jana time to push him off Tomen.

She slapped Tomen across the face.

"Tomen, wake up. Please, my love. Don't leave me."

Tomen opened his eyes briefly and saw Amar sprawled on the floor; the knife was next to Tomen.

"Please don't die," Jana begged; her dressing gown covered in his blood.

"I'm… so…sorry Jan. I love you," Tomen said

"I love you too."

Just then, Tomen saw from the corner of his eyes Amar getting up. Tomen moved his hand to pick up the knife and whispered into Jana's ears.

"Move."

Jana moved out of the way in time and just then Amar threw himself on Tomen and onto the knife in Tomen's hands. Jana watched in horror as the knife pierced Amar's neck with his eyes gazing straight at Tomen. But Tomen wasn't moving. She screamed at the top of her voice because she could tell he was gone.

Jana moved Amar away from Tomen and his blood spilled everywhere.

This wasn't meant to happen.

Jana cursed the day she ever laid eyes on Amar but that was the same day she had met Tomen.

"You had to go and die; you had to go and leave me alone. Tomen, we just started, we just… started our lives together. You promised me you wouldn't die. Tomen you promised and now you have left me in this cruel world by myself," Jana lamented, throwing herself on his body

Jana cried until nothing else came from her eyes. The pain of Tomen's death consumed her whole soul and nothing mattered anymore.

Jana didn't know how long she laid on his body for but she heard footsteps and knew that whoever it was planned to take him away from her. Jana clung to his body as two men reached for her and pulled her way from him.

"Please, come with us," she heard someone say.

"No, I can't leave him. I can't leave him by himself. He will be cold without me. Please, please, I beg you, let me stay with him," Jana shouted, disorientated.

"I'm sorry," she heard another person say. They started to discuss the scene as they took her out of the room into an ambulance. Jana didn't know who called the police or the ambulance.

"Are you hurt anywhere ma'am?".

"I don't know. But this is not my blood. I need to go back to Tomen, he needs me. Please let me go back. I can't leave him, he needs me. She continued to lament.

"I'm sorry," a woman said. "We need to check you out." Just then, Jana saw two bodies covered in black being wheeled out of the house and she ran towards the bodies.

"Please tell me, which one is Tomen? Which one is my husband?" Jana tried to pull off the cover but someone held her back. "No leave me alone, I can't leave him on his own, I have to go with him please. Let me go with him."

"First, you need to come with us, then when you are okay and his body has been examined and prepared by an examiner, we will let you see him," The woman with her said, speaking softly.

Just then she saw Omar, Tomen's head of security.

"This is all your fault. Your wife gave Amar our address and access to our house. Tomen died because you didn't do your job. You killed him, it's your fault he's dead. And it's all your fault," Jana shouted, throwing her fist against his chest.

Two people peeled her away from Omar and led her away into the ambulance.

Jana screamed, kicked her feet and shouted until she was sedated.

As she closed her eyes, she wished never to wake again. Nothing was worth living for but Tomen had made her promise she wouldn't kill herself and she knew she had to at least honour his life by somehow finding a purpose to live on for.

Chapter Fourteen

Tears spilled down Jana's face as she forced the memories of her life with Tomen away. This was her purpose in life now to stop this evil from repeating itself in Nina's life. Jana wiped her tears as she pulled her thoughts back into the present.

Binta was just as cold-hearted as their parents but Jana knew there was a reason, she chose to stay alive after Tomen's death; she wasn't going to sit idly by and let Nina's happiness slip away from her.

Jana got a text on her phone and it was Nina, telling her where they were.

Jana got in her car and drove to the hotel Laura had picked out for them. Jana knocked on the door and was met with an embrace from Nina.

"Aunty I'm glad you're here. Please talk to Jon's mum, she's freaking out." Nina looked panicked.

Jana sighed. She had spoken to Laura about supporting the kids but she wasn't ready for this back and forth.

"What is it now Laura?" Jana asked the moment she put her bag down on the table in the hotel.

"I don't think your plan will work. I mean I support them but I've got a very bad feeling and I can't shake it. Please give them their daughter. It's the only way I know to ensure Jon's safety."

"Mum, you need to stop this. I made up my mind. This is my path in life now. My life is with Nina and if I have to tell you that a million times until you get it, I will. I'm not leaving her and we are done doing this with you. We are going to get married. Get on board or not but it is happening," Jon declared.

"You don't know what you're saying. Do you know how it felt for me to watch your life hang on a balance? I mean no disrespect Nina but if you truly care about him like you say, you will walk away from him. You will tell him to go and live his life. Love doesn't always mean happiness; it means making the best decision for each other and that is that you path ways. I mean, yes you love each other but it's not the end of the world. You can actually survive without each other if you both do this for your own safety. She will be alive in her new life and you will make a life for yourself but you will be alive and that is all I want for you Jon. I want you to live. I don't want a life where you are constantly watching your back and if you had any sense, you would tell them the same. Don't fill their heads with this fantasy about some insane love. Who has it worked out for? I loved your father very much but still he left us alone and never looked back. The type of love you all talk about only exists in movies but in the real world, we need to face reality. Things are different and don't always work out the way we want and we need to make adjustments and do the best we can. And the best thing for the two of you is to split. I don't want this for you; I don't support it. In fact, I forbid you to marry her Jon. I forbid you to join yourself to anyone that is related to that vile family. And if you carry on, then you are on your own, do you hear me Jon." Laura picked up her bag and walked towards Jon.

Jana shook her head because she didn't know what to do. Laura was right, her sister and her husband were vile, but that wasn't Nina's fault. She wanted to help but then perhaps Laura was right. What if Jon is killed like her Tomen was murdered.

"If you know what's good for you and If I'm still your mother, you will come with me now and put an end to all of this nonsense."

"Mum, you've made your decision and I made mine a long time ago. I'm marrying Nina and as long as she wants me in her life, she will always be the girl for me," Jon said.

Laura scoffed, "I hope we all don't regret this. I'm going back home." She started to walk out and stopped beside Jana.

"If any harm comes to my son, I will tear down all your family. That's a promise. You tell that to your sister."

Jana watched as Laura left the room.

"What are we going to do now?" Nina asked her aunt.

"We go tomorrow and book a date at the registry. If this is what you both want, then I will support you no matter what. But we have to be careful because as much as it pains me to say this, my sister and her husband are like wounded lions. When we get back from the registry, we go to the police and tell them everything, in case anything happens - not that it will. I mean I hope it doesn't get to that. Um lastly, I know someone who can provide security. Until I find a place that is safe for you both to live, you will have bodyguards and you must go with them anywhere you go. They will keep you both safe."

"Thank you, Aunty, thank you for sticking by us," Nina said.

"Yeah, I don't know how to thank you. I appreciate everything you are doing for Nina and I," Jon said

"Don't mention it," Jana said softly. "I'll see you both tomorrow. You can stay here in this hotel; I will pay for a few more weeks. I would take you back home to mine but they may have someone staking out my house. So, this is the safest option for now. Order in room service - anything you want but don't go overboard. Also, don't leave until I get the security to you, okay. And one last thing, you might want to decide between you both where you want to relocate to. We need to stay two steps ahead."

Jon and Nina smiled in appreciation.

"Okay goodnight."

"Goodnight Aunty," both Jon and Nina chorused.

Jana picked up her bag and walked away from her niece. She hoped she was doing the best thing for the two of them. What Laura wanted was to keep them both safe but that meant they would both live miserable lives. *If only she could get through to Binta and make her see sense*, Jana thought as she drove back home.

Chapter Fifteen

Jana laid on her bed and quickly dozed off. She was emotionally exhausted and once more Tomen had appeared next to her in her dreams. The past two days since Nina called had been so hectic and she was glad to be back in the arms of Tomen. But this time around, something was wrong. Tomen was saying something to her and his face looked worried but Jana couldn't make sense of the words his mouth was forming. He had always just held her in the past but this time he was saying something that worried him.

Jana woke up with a start because she felt uneasy then her phone rang as though on cue.

She picked it up while, her heart raced within her.

"Aunty!" Nina whispered into the phone. Jana could hear the terror in her voice

"Nina! What's wrong?" Jana asked

"They took him - they beat him up and took him."

Jana was quiet. She hadn't expected that they would find them so quickly.

"How? How did they know where you were?"

Nina sniffed, "I don't know Aunty. They are going to kill him. Please go to the police Aunty. Please."

"Okay, okay. Where are you?"

"I ran while they were walking me down to the lobby. I just kept running aunty. But I'm afraid for Jon. You need to help us."

"Okay, Okay. I will call the police now. But tell me where you are and I will come get you," Jana said.

"No Aunty, I need to go back for Jon."

"Don't be stupid. If you go back, they will have the two of you," Jana explained.

"I know but what can I do? I can't abandon him. He won't abandon me," Nina cried into the phone.

"It's my fault. I shouldn't have left you two in the hotel by yourself."

"It's not your fault Aunty, don't blame yourself. You tried and only you understand what I'm going through."

"Nina tell me where you are, I'll come get you."

"No Aunty, they are probably following you. They must have tailed you to the hotel. How else would they know where to find us," Nina said.

"Yeah! Probably," Jana agreed remorsefully.

"Call the police now and with any luck, they will find him if they look through the CCTV. I don't have enough battery on my phone," Nina said.

"Yes, you are right. I will call them now," Jana assured.

She dialled the police and explained the situation as she knew it to them. That was another fifteen minutes. When she was done, she called Binta's phone with no success. Jana felt useless because she didn't know what to do to help. She wished she had listened to Laura and convinced Jon to go home with his mum. Now, she wasn't sure what would happen to Jon. If they had tried before with no success, they would want to finish the job now. This only reminded her of what happened to Tomen. This was her fault, Jana decided. Why did she encourage their love? Why did she make them feel like they could do as they wanted and now that poor boy's life could be lost? She called Binta and Aalim's phone again but no one picked up. She called the police, who assured her they were on it and that she should just sit back and wait. Time crawled along; Jana tried calling Nina's phone but she was sent to voicemail. Sighing loudly, she knew Nina's phone was dead.

When it was seven in the morning, finally her doorbell rang and Jana ran to open the door. She expected it to be Nina but two policemen stood outside her door and Jana could tell by the looks on their faces, it wasn't happy news.

"What happened officers, did you find my niece and her boyfriend?"

"May we come in?"

Jana quickly stepped out of the way.

"Please don't keep me waiting. Did you find them?"

"No, we didn't find your niece but… we found the body of a man closely matching the one you described. He had been killed."

Laura felt her legs giving way and her body reaching for the ground. One of the officers caught her before she did harm to herself. They lead her to a chair and waited a while for her to feel better.

"Do you have anyone with you?"

Jana looked about aimlessly. "Yeah! My house staff will arrive soon." Tears rolled down Jana's face.

"I told them they could do this; I told them their love mattered. I should have warned them about the bitter end of love. I mean this type of love that only plagues the heart. Laura warned us all and she wanted her boy to come with her. I didn't listen to her; I wanted those kids to be happy. I should have listened. Now what do I say to that poor woman. That her son, her only child, her world has been killed by the evil men of this world."

"Madam, do you have any idea where we can find his mum?"

"No, she said she was leaving yesterday. She left to go back to Manchester. She wanted to take him because she said she had a bad feeling. She should have done so. Now she will never see him again and it's my fault. All my fault."

"How do you mean?" one of the officers asked.

"It's my fault. I told them it was okay to be in love, I told them I would support them," she wailed.

"Do you know who's responsible?"

"I don't know who exactly killed that boy but my sister and her husband are behind it. They are the ones who wanted to force their daughter into an arranged marriage. They are the ones those kids were running away from and they may not have physically killed him but they probably paid someone to do it." She wept. "What about my niece, any news of her?" Jana requested.

"No, nothing so far. We are looking and using all the resources we have to try to locate her. We will find her, I promise."

Just then Jana's phone rang.

"You will excuse me for a minute." Jana picked up the call.

It was Nina.

"Aunty," she cried into the phone.

"Nina!" Jana yelled happily. "Where are you? I've been so worried."

"I told you Aunty, I'm looking for Jon"

"I know Nina, but come home first, we will do it together."

"No Aunty, there is a police barricade not far from the hotel and people are saying someone was stabbed to death. I need to know it's not Jon. Aunty, have you heard anything. Has anyone mentioned anything?"

Jana was quiet because she didn't know what to say.

"Do you have Laura's number?" Jana asked.

"Yes, what do you need it for? Aunty, tell me was it him, was it… Jon?"

"Come home to me Nina, please."

"You're not answering me Aunty. Is Jon okay? Is he okay Aunty? Tell me please, tell me the truth," Nina screamed into the phone.

"Nina please, I don't… I don't know."

"You're lying to me. It's him isn't it? It's Jon. They killed him. Well you can tell my mum she got her way but I can't be here no more. Not without Jon."

"What do you mean Nina? What do you mean by that? I can help you, just come back home."

"Thanks Aunty. Please look after my sisters, they will need you. I have to go now."

"Nina! Nina! Please don't do anything foolish."

"Goodbye Aunty, I love you," Nina said and hung up. Jana turned to the officers who must have heard what just transpired between her and her niece.

"You've got to help me please. Don't just stand there doing nothing. You've got to help me. That was my niece. She's going to kill herself. Please help me save her," Jana yelled.

"Do you know where she's at now?" Jana shook her head.

"She mentioned she was at the partition near where Jon's body was found. Can you please call to see if anyone has seen her, I beg you. Please stop her before she does anything foolish to herself."

"Don't worry, we will call around to see if anyone see someone matching her description."

One of the officers moved away to do a radio call, then a dispatch call came through.

"Yes, okay. We are close to the precinct. We will get there right away," the officer said into his radio.

"Sorry maam but we need to go now."

"What is it? Is it Nina?" Jana asked, scared out of her senses.

"We don't know but we will update you if we hear anything about your niece."

The officers quickly walked out the door. Jana followed closely and she heard the officer saying something to each other about an accident.

Jana quickly picked up her car keys because she wasn't just going to sit down and do nothing.

She followed the police car closely as they blared through the streets. The accident was close to the hotel and Jana's heart sank. Her greatest fear was coming through. She parked her car and ran towards the point of accident; a girl was lying on the floor with her body twisted about. Jana knew immediately it was Nina.

She ran towards her niece but the police and the paramedics held her back.

"No! Let me go, that's… my niece. That's my Nina!" Jana yelled.

She broke free and went over to look at Nina's body. The officers who had been in her house, told their colleagues to leave her alone.

"Let her have a moment with her," one of the officers whispered.

"You foolish girl, why?! Why did you do this to yourself? Why did you leave me?" Jana knelt on the floor, pulling Nina's body to her.

Nina's eyes were still opened. Blood ran down the side of her face to her back. She wasn't breathing, whatever she did she made sure it took her life quickly. Jana stared at her for a moment and then placed her hands over her eyes to close them. Her tears spilled over to Nina's face.

"Sleep now my darling, sleep my little angel and say hello to Jon and Tomen for me. It won't be long now;

I will live on for all of us and then one day it will be my turn." Jana kissed Nina on her forehead.

"Goodnight my beautiful girl."

An officer came and pulled her away.

"They have to take her body now," the woman whispered and Jana looked up with her eyes completely blinded by tears. Jana nodded and gently placed Nina's body down gently.

She looked at the officer, "Thank you," she whispered.

"Don't mention it."

"My sister and her husband are to be blamed for this tragic death too, you must find and punish them to the full extent of the law. Promise me you will do that for me and for these poor souls," Jana pleaded.

"I will do my best, at least if not for Nina, then for Jon," The officer assured.

"Thank you."

"We can't let you drive home in this state. Come with us, we will take you back home. Someone will drive your car back home for you," the officer said.

Jana followed the officers into their car.

She was silent all the way home as she still couldn't believe what had happened.

In her bid to save her niece, she had ensured her death.

The officers dropped her home and Jana waved them goodbye before walking into her home. She met one of her house staff in the hallway, who greeted Jana.

"I'm going to my room. I won't be available all day," Jana said.

"But you have a visitor." Jana raised her brow.

"I'm in no state to see anyone."

"It's your sister."

Jana stopped in her tracks. "Where is she?"

"She's in the sitting room."

"Okay thank you," Jana said and walked towards the sitting room.

She saw Binta standing with her back turned to her.

"What are you doing back here Binta," Jana asked.

"I need your help."

"It's too late for that; for anything as a matter of fact."

"What do you mean?"

"You had that boy killed."

"I didn't. I told Aalim to tell them to only scare him."

"Well, they did more than that and you can try to put all the blame on your husband but you are both equally at fault. You could have been a better mother to your daughter. Now, you've killed that poor beautiful boy. What shall you say to his mother? This was not the first time you tried to kill him, so don't come here looking for pity Binta."

"I swear to you Jana, I have no hand in this."

"Save it for the police: it's not me you need to convince. I already know who you are and in my assessment of you, you are a cruel heartless woman and do not deserve the beautiful children God gifted you with."

"You don't mean that Jana. I am your sister. Yes, I can be stubborn and I do say pretty mean things when I'm angry but I'm still your sister."

"No, you're not. You may be related to me by blood but you don't get to call yourself my sister. We are not family."

Binta was quiet.

"Okay, have it your way. Have you heard from Nina? She will need her mum at this difficult time," Binta said.

Jana shook her head. "Yes, I did hear from Nina. She called this morning. That poor beautiful girl. When she found out that you and her father had murdered the man she loved, she was overwhelmed by such sadness that she decided, she couldn't…"

"What are you saying Jana," Binta cut in.

"I'm telling you what happened. What your stubbornness caused. Nina died this morning; she threw herself in front of a moving van."

"No, you're lying. You witch, you're lying. Nina wouldn't do that to herself. My daughter wouldn't kill herself; she's stronger than that."

"Well, you got what you wanted Binta."

"What do you mean? I never wanted this; how cruel can you be. How can you say that?"

"Because, you saw how forcing two people in love apart shattered my world. I'm alive only because I promised Tomen, I would live for the two us. You saw how tragically devastating my world collapsed. For years, I was nothing more than a shell and you inflicted that same pain on your own daughter, simply because she loved someone you didn't approve of. So yes, you got what you wanted since you refused to learn from the past mistakes of our parents."

Binta broke down where she was and wept.

"One more thing. I won't let you do the same to the rest of your girls. I will do everything in my powers to see they are all taken from you. Now you may see yourself out of my house Binta. I need to lie down," Jana said walking to her room.

Jana sat and thought about the last 72 hours. She knew she did her best but wished she had known that these kids would die. She wouldn't have even allowed them to come to her. Perhaps if they were still on the run, they would still both be alive. Another set of tears spilled down her face. Jana wiped them away, laid down and shut her eyes. She was dying inside and only Tomen could help heal her broken heart. *How could love not bring anything but pain*, Jana thought. If she had not loved Tomen, he would probably still be alive. However, even with all the heartaches and pain that plagued her, Jana knew it was better to have loved and lost, than not to know the beautiful intensity and purity that comes with such love.

Soon, sleep claimed her and once again, Tomen welcomed her into his embrace.

She stared at him.

"It's okay. They are together now," she heard him say.

Jana smiled; Tomen was now speaking to her.

"I miss you," she said.

He smiled and curled her into his arms.

The end